PROTECTING JULIE

A SEAL OF PROTECTION NOVELLA

SUSAN STOKER

Julie Lytle is working hard to turn her life around. Being kidnapped by sex traffickers changed her drastically, but having grown up the spoiled daughter of a senator, Julie wishes she could've changed just a little sooner. Shamed by her behavior toward the woman rescued alongside her, and further embarrassed and guilt-racked over the way she treated the SEALs who risked their lives on her behalf, Julie is desperate to make amends.

With help from a D.C. acquaintance who'd endured her own harrowing experience, Julie connects with Patrick Hurt, Commander of the SEALs who'd saved her life. If she can prove she's not the same person who mistreated his team, he'll grant her request to meet them—but not before the protective, sexy man makes a surprising request of his own.

**Protecting Julie is a part of the SEAL of Protection Series. It can be read as a stand-alone, but it's recommended you read the books in order to get maximum enjoyment out of the series.

CHAPTER 1

JULIE SAT UP IN BED AND GASPED IN FRIGHT, THROWING herself off the side of her double bed and landing on her hands and knees on the floor with a thud. She immediately scuttled to the nearby wall and collapsed against it, curling into a small ball. Her arms went around her legs and squeezed even as she buried her head into her knees and sobbed.

It'd been almost a month since she'd dreamt she was back in Mexico. Julie had hoped the nightmares had stopped for good, but it was obvious that moving across the country to California and starting her life over wasn't the magic cure-all to make them stop. She loved her daddy with all her heart and knew everything he'd done was out of concern and love for *her*, but she'd thought that maybe she was still dreaming about the hell she went through because she was living in the house she'd grown up in and in the town where she'd been kidnapped. She was twenty-eight years old, more than old enough to move out of her father's house and be on her own.

But at that moment, remembering what had happened to her, she wished she was back in her daddy's house, where she'd always felt safe, even with the continued nightmares. Julie knew it didn't make sense...she moved to California to try to get away from the nightmares, but even when she was at home she knew she could wake up her daddy and he'd talk to her and comfort her until she felt better.

She was a completely different person now than the naïve young woman who'd been kidnapped and almost sold into a prostitution ring south of the border about a year and a half ago. Julie didn't like to remember how she'd acted when the Navy SEAL had found and rescued her.

Truth of the matter was, she'd been terrified, frightened out of her skull, and she'd lashed out at the woman who'd been held in the same hellhole, and who'd handled everything that had happened to them a thousand percent better than Julie had.

Julie forced air into her lungs slowly, remembering what her therapist had told her. When she was overwhelmed and felt the panic attacks coming on, she needed to concentrate on breathing. In. Out. In. Out. Slowly but surely, Julie felt her heart rate slow and the adrenaline coursing through her body start to wane.

She stood up and braced herself on the mattress as she made her way around the end of her bed into the small bathroom attached to the equally small bedroom. Julie splashed some water on her face and steadied herself with her hands on the counter. The water dripped from her chin as she looked in the mirror.

What she saw made her wince. She had lines furrowed in her forehead. Her eyes were slightly bloodshot and her short brown hair hung around her face. Her cheeks were sunken in and even though she knew she'd gained the weight back from her time spent in the hands of the kidnappers, but because of the nightmares and the fact that she wasn't eating well, even all these months after she was rescued, she was still too skinny.

Her five-foot-two frame was naturally small, but now, at a little over a hundred pounds, she looked even more fragile.

"Get it together, Julie," she told herself in a firm voice, glaring at her reflection. She sighed and reached for the towel hanging on the rack next to the utilitarian bathtub/shower combo. She dried her face and headed back into the bedroom, straightened the covers and climbed back into bed.

Julie thought about her plans for the next day, sure they were why she'd had the nightmare. It was time. She'd put it off for way too long, but it was finally time.

After she'd gotten back home from Mexico, and after a few visits with a therapist her dad had scheduled visits for her with, Julie knew she had to find the SEAL team that had rescued her so she could thank them. But no matter how much she'd begged her dad, he'd claimed he had no way of getting ahold of the SEALs and had suggested she should move on with her life.

Ironically, it had been one of her acquaintances who had given her the information she'd needed so she *could* get on with living.

————

Stacey Kellogg was the daughter of a senator who worked with Julie's dad. She knew Stacey from all the political parties they'd attended with their families. They'd belonged to the same country club in

Virginia and had even played tennis together a couple of times in the past.

Julie had been horrified when she'd learned Stacey had been kidnapped by an ex-boyfriend. He apparently decided that if she wasn't with him, he didn't want her being with anyone. He went on the run with her for a week and a half. Julie didn't know all the details of what she went through, but what she had heard, it had been a harrowing ordeal for her.

The fact that they'd both been held against their will was what gave Julie the strength to approach Stacey. Even though their situations weren't exactly the same, she figured she and the other woman shared something unique. She'd sought Stacey out at the club a few months ago, before moving to California. Stacey had been eating, and Julie had approached and traded some superficial greetings, then asked if it'd be okay to talk to Stacey alone.

They'd moved off to a group of comfortable easy chairs in the corner of the large lounge and they'd spoken for over an hour. Julie knew Stacey was dating a Navy SEAL, who'd been involved in her ultimate rescue, and hoped he'd be able to somehow assist her in finding the SEALs who'd helped her. Stacey hadn't promised anything, but said she'd ask her boyfriend, Diesel Bonds. They'd exchanged phone numbers and when Julie didn't hear anything for a week, figured Stacey had blown her off.

But when Stacey had texted her and asked to meet, Julie was shocked, but pleased. They'd gotten together at a restaurant, and Julie had been surprised to see a gorgeous man with Stacey.

After they'd sat down at a small table, Stacey said happily, "Hey, Julie, it's good to see you again."

"Hi, Stacey. You too."

"This is Diesel. We talked about him last week."

Julie nodded and held out her hand. "It's good to meet you. Thank you for your service. I know those words are somewhat cliché, but I mean them from the bottom of my heart."

"You're welcome."

Diesel shook her hand, then returned his arm to the back of Stacey's chair. It was a protective posture, and Julie couldn't help but envy her for having a man who wanted to shield her from anything and anyone who might cause her harm.

Stacey didn't beat around the bush. "You said you wanted to know who rescued you."

Julie nodded and pressed her lips together nervously.

"Why?" It was Diesel who asked.

"Because I was a bitch." Julie laid it all out on the table. "There I was in the middle of the Mexican jungle. I'd been violated, I hurt, I was hungry and scared out of my skull. This guy came into the hut I'd been shoved in. He surprised me, and I acted like he was trying to pick me up at a bar." She shook her head in disgust, remembering her actions that day in the jungle.

"There was another woman there. She'd been there a lot longer than me, and seeing her, freaked me out. I knew that could be me. When I finally understood how long she'd been there, I realized how screwed I really was. So I lashed out. I was rude and bitchy. All I wanted was out of the jungle and out of the country. I wanted to be home. I'm embarrassed to admit that, even hurt and hooked on drugs, the other woman was acting so much better than me, it wasn't even a comparison. Even the SEAL thought so. And that made me think that maybe he'd decide I was too much trouble, and he'd leave me in the jungle. It was a stupid thing to think; of course he wasn't going to leave me there. But it made me act even bitchier."

Julie lowered her eyes, embarrassed. Her voice dropped to a whisper, "I'm ashamed that I didn't even thank them. His team showed up with a helicopter, the SEAL was hurt as we were hauled up into the chopper, and I didn't even bother to turn around and say 'are you all right' or 'thank you.' Not to any of them."

"What makes you think that they want to hear your thanks?" Diesel asked without rancor.

Julie looked up at the hard man in front of her. She avoided Stacey's gaze. She forced herself to keep eye contact with Diesel. "I'm sure they don't. I know they were all glad to see the last of me. I can only imagine their conversations once I was gone. I know it's selfish, but I need to do this. I..." Julie's voice trailed off, not sure what she could say that this super SEAL sitting in front of her would understand.

"I don't know what team got you out. It wasn't SEAL Team Six; that much I know. We don't talk about our missions; even within the brotherhood, they're top secret. But I know a guy. His name is Tex. He lives out here in Virginia. He used to be a SEAL, but was medically retired after losing part of his leg in a mission. I'll call him. See if he knows who was on the team that rescued you. He seems to know everything about everyone. But, Julie, I can't guarantee he'll tell me."

Julie sat up straighter in her chair. "I know, but I appreciate you even asking. Seriously. I know I'm still being selfish. No one in their right mind would want to see me again after the way I acted, but I swear I'm a different person now," she said earnestly.

"You don't have to convince me, Julie," Diesel said gently. "People can be unpredictable in hostage and rescue situations. You probably remember it worse than it really was."

"I don't think so," Julie said honestly. "I was pretty horrible."

"Hey, I heard you're moving?" Stacey asked, trying to move them on from the uncomfortable topic.

"Yeah. I can't stay here any longer. I love my dad, but it's time for me to move on. I can't stand politics, and my dad loves it, of course. I feel smothered living in his house. I need to get out, do something useful with my life. Being in charge of his house and being a hostess for his political parties just isn't fulfilling anymore. I need to...give back."

"Give back?"

Julie tried to explain, "Uh-huh. I feel like I've gotten a new lease on life. Those men found me and gave me a chance to be a better person. I blew it with them, but I'm ready to prove that I'm not the selfish bitch I was down there, and that I'm pretty sure I was before I was kidnapped."

"I'm sure you weren't that bitchy," Diesel protested.

"Thanks, but yeah, I was." Julie said ruefully. "While I wish I could move across the country and earn my own living without any help from anyone, I know I can't. So my dad is helping. But my idea is to move out to California and start my own nonprofit agency."

"Really? Isn't that harder than it sounds? Don't you have to have a business degree or something?"

Julie nodded. "Yeah, probably. But as I said, my dad is helping. He has some friends out there who will be helping me with the paperwork, marketing, and the day-to-day running of the business. He's gonna pay them until I can get my business on its feet and take over the payroll."

"What will you be doing?"

"I was watching one of the daytime talk shows and got the idea. I have a knack for fashion, so I want to see if I can start a thrift store of sorts, but full of designer clothes. I figure lots of women out in California are rich and probably have dresses and clothes they don't wear anymore. I want to get them to donate them to my secondhand store. I could sell as much as possible and also give outfits to people who need nice dressy clothes for interviews. The money I raise after paying expenses I could donate to various programs to help struggling women."

There was silence around the table for a beat before Julie hurried to say, "I know, it's kinda stupid, but I couldn't think of—"

"It's not stupid," Stacey said quickly. "I think it's awesome. It's a great idea."

"Well, it's not like I'm doing it by myself. I need my dad's money to start it up and the people he knows to help me, but I'm hoping that once I learn more about it, I'll be able to contribute more as time goes by and eventually be one hundred percent responsible for the day-to-day expenses."

"I think it's a wonderful idea," Stacey said resolutely.

"Thanks." Julie looked up in relief as the waitress approached the table. The conversation had gotten pretty awkward for her.

They ordered sandwiches and there was no more talk about SEALs, rescues or charities as they ate their lunch. As they were leaving, Diesel shook Julie's hand and held on when she would've pulled back.

"I wasn't there when you were being rescued, but I wanted to say, if you do get to meet the SEALs who helped you, let them see the woman who ate lunch with us today. They'll forgive you."

"Do you really think so?" Julie's voice was low and worried.

"Yeah."

"Thanks, Diesel."

"You're welcome. Don't forget to stay in touch with Stacey and let her know how things go for you out there in California."

Julie looked at Stacey. "I'd like that."

"Me too," Stacey agreed. "Good luck with everything."

"Thanks."

Julie watched as Stacey and Diesel walked across the parking lot to his sports car. She observed Diesel opening the passenger door and waiting for Stacey to get settled. Julie sighed. In her old life, Julie might've been jealous and catty and would've tried to flirt and steal Diesel from Stacey. But not now. They were a great couple, and while Julie might've been jealous of their obviously close relationship, she was also happy for Stacey.

It was great that Stacey seemed to be moving on after her kidnapping, Julie smiled and waved as Diesel pulled out of the restaurant parking lot.

Julie had packed up her small SUV and left

Virginia to drive across the country a week later. She still hadn't heard from Diesel or anyone named Tex, but she couldn't wait for them to get ahold of her. It was time to start her new life out in California.

It had been a month and a half since she'd arrived in Riverton before she'd finally heard from the man Diesel had called Tex. Her phone had rung, and even though the number said "unknown," Julie had answered it anyway.

"Hello?"

"Is this Julie Lytle?"

"Yes, who's this?"

"My name is Tex. I heard from Diesel Bonds that you had some questions about your rescue?"

The voice on the other end of the line was deep with a southern accent. He almost sounded bored. Julie's heart immediately started beating faster.

"Yes. I wanted to thank the men who came all the way to Mexico to rescue me."

"They would've done the same thing for anyone."

Julie winced. Wow, this Tex guy didn't pull any punches. "I know. But I...I was mean. And I feel bad. I didn't say thank you when the men dropped me off, and I wanted to make sure they knew I'm thankful for all they did."

"I can't tell you the names of the men," Tex said bluntly.

Julie's heart dropped. "Oh, okay."

"But I can give you the phone number of their Commander. You can talk to him and if he thinks it's appropriate, he'll get you in touch with the SEALs."

"Okay. Yeah, that sounds great," Julie enthused.

"I'm not sure I'd get too excited," Tex warned. "Commander Hurt's awfully protective of the men under his command. If I had to say, I'd give you a thirty/seventy shot of being able to thank the men in person. Hurt will probably tell you he'll pass the message on for you."

"It's better than no chance," Julie said resolutely.

Tex laughed under his breath. "Optimistic."

"Yeah, it's more than I had this time yesterday."

"True."

"I...thank you."

"Don't thank me," Tex chuckled. "You still have a hard road ahead of you."

Julie straightened her spine. "I can do it."

"Good luck. Now. Got a pen?"

Julie fumbled with her purse and got out a pen and a receipt from a fast food restaurant she'd eaten lunch at that day. "Ready."

Tex gave her a phone number and once again wished her luck.

———

Now Julie was lying in bed, thinking back over the last month and a half and all that had changed in her life, and trying to recover from the nightmare and subsequent panic attack she'd had earlier. Tomorrow she'd call this Commander Hurt guy and get him to agree to let her talk to the SEALs who rescued her. No problem.

She closed her eyes and tried to relax. Tried to pretend that she wasn't as nervous as she'd ever been in her life. As the sun rose in the sky, Julie was no closer to being relaxed than when she first woke up from her nightmare.

CHAPTER 2

"Hello?"

"Uh, hi. My name is Julie and—"

"How'd you get this number?" Patrick Hurt wasn't often surprised, but to hear a soft feminine voice on the other end of his work phone was out of the norm. And he didn't like abnormal.

"Tex gave it to me. My name is Julie Lytle—"

"Tex? Why the hell would Tex give you my number?"

"If you'd let me talk, I'll tell you."

Patrick barely held back the snort of laughter that threatened to escape. It'd been a long time since he'd been spoken to with such...snark. As the Commander of an elite SEAL team, he'd gotten used to being treated with respect. "By all means then...

tell me." He heard the woman take a deep breath before she continued.

"As I was saying, my name is Julie Lytle. I got your number from Tex. I wanted to thank the Navy SEALs who rescued me from a hellacious situation, and Tex told me you were their Commander. I know you probably can't give me their names, but I'd like to meet them and thank them in person for saving my life."

"No."

"I'd appreciate...uh... No?"

"That's right. No. The missions the SEALs undertake are top secret. It would be against protocol for them to be jaunting to meet-and-greets so they could be thanked. It's their job, ma'am. That's all."

"First of all, I get that what they do is top secret, but since I was *there*, it's not secret to *me*. And secondly, I don't care if it *is* their job, this was the first time I had to be saved, and it wasn't just a job to *me*. Thirdly, I'll flat out say it—I was a bitch and I need to make it right."

Patrick sat back in his chair in his office and ran a hand through his dark hair. He didn't need this shit today. "Look, Julie, was it? I'm glad they saved you, I am, really. But don't you think the fact you were a bitch would mean they don't want to see you or get your thanks?"

"Yes," she immediately returned, and Patrick's respect for the mysterious woman rose a notch. She continued. "I know they don't want it, but they deserve it. I swear I won't be obnoxious, I won't fawn all over them. I won't go to the press. We can meet in a back alley somewhere if that makes you more comfortable. I just..." Her voice trailed off.

Patrick didn't say anything, letting the silence stretch, and as he expected, she started talking again to fill the awkward break in conversation.

"I was about to be sold to a bunch of really scary guys. They'd already taught me what to expect when I was sold, and let me tell you, the thought of being a receptacle for who the hell knows how many men's lust wasn't a good one. Your team saved me from a fate worse than death and I just want to look them in the eye and say 'thank you for giving me my life back.'"

Patrick clenched his teeth and mentally swore. Julie Lytle. The name clicked with the mission she was talking about.

He'd heard a lot about the infamous Julie, and she was right, she *had* been a bitch. He knew Cookie and the others wouldn't really want to hear her thanks. They were glad to deliver her into her father's arms and see the last of her. Not to mention, Patrick didn't think Fiona needed the reminder of what had happened. The last thing he wanted was to put her in a position where she'd have another flashback.

But there was...sincerity...in Julie's voice that he hadn't heard from many other victims and people they'd rescued. Patrick was a pretty good judge of character, he had to be after being a SEAL himself and now commanding the team from behind the scenes.

"Julie. Yeah, I remember you, and I have to be honest. I don't think the guys would want to see you again."

"Oh. Okay." Julie's voice was soft and Patrick could tell she was on the verge of tears. "I appreciate you taking the time to talk to me anyway. If it's not too much to ask, could you at least tell them I called and thank them *for* me? It's not the same, but it's better than nothing."

Patrick made a split-second decision that he hoped he wouldn't regret. "Thursday afternoon. Four o'clock. I'll meet you and we can talk about it. If I think you're honestly sincere and you're doing this for the right reasons, I'll consider letting you meet the men."

"I'll be there. Where are we meeting?"

"Pacific Beach up by La Jolla."

"Okay. How will I—"

"I'll find you," Patrick told her, knowing what she was going to ask. He could find out what she looked like easily enough. It wasn't as if her kidnapping was a secret. It'd been all over the media after she'd returned home.

"Great. I'll see you there in a couple of days then. And Commander Hurt? Thank you. Seriously. You don't know what this means to me."

"Thursday. See you later."

"Bye."

"Bye."

Patrick hung up his phone and put his hands on the back of his head and leaned back in his chair. He wasn't a man who generally liked surprises, and he'd just had a whopper of one dropped in his lap. He didn't really have a plan, but he'd play it by ear. Once again the SEAL motto came to his mind. *The only easy day was yesterday.* How true.

Julie smiled as she hung up the phone. She knew it wasn't a done deal, but she felt on top of the world. Meeting with the SEAL Commander brought her one step closer to being able to move on and right the huge wrong she'd done. All she had to do was meet up with the SEALs, then she'd really be able to put the entire episode behind her and concentrate on her new life.

In the past month, she'd worked harder than she ever had before, and she was loving every second of it. She'd scoped out the country clubs and made pitches to several women's groups. The two women and one man her father had found to help her were wonderful.

They'd helped her find the cutest little storefront in Mission Valley. She'd had a logo designed and the store decorated. There were comfortable chairs scattered around the inside for customers or their spouses to sit in. She put in a free little coffee bar, so shoppers could get a snack and a drink. The clothes were all professionally cleaned and displayed after being donated. It honestly looked like a small boutique instead of the secondhand store that it was.

Business had been really good. Julie knew she'd been successful so far because of the help she'd gotten from her dad, but she'd also worked her butt off. She'd spent most of her day either meeting with people to drum up interest, or networking. She'd also gone around the area to other thrift stores scouring the racks for designer clothes she could purchase and fill her own racks with.

Julie hoped with the amount of connections she was making she could continue to grow and garner interest in her venture. She'd spoken with a few managers of some battered women's shelters in the area and had a meeting set up for the following week with a woman who ran one of the local Boys and Girls Clubs. There was also a teen center Julie wanted to check into as well. She'd expanded her idea of donating interview clothes to women in need, to also wanting to donate fancy dresses for teenagers who couldn't afford to buy one for their prom.

The bell over the shop door tinkled as three women entered. Julie put aside her excitement over being able to speak to Commander Hurt in a few days and turned to the women to give them her welcome spiel.

"Hello, welcome to *My Sister's Closet*, feel free to look around. All the clothes have been donated and are the real thing. Versace, Hermès, Ralph Lauren, Prada, Kate Spade, Chanel, Gucci...you name it, we have it. I think you'll find the prices very reasonable. If you have any questions, feel free to ask. Dressing rooms are in the back, and help yourself to a cup of coffee if you'd like."

The women nodded politely at her and wandered over to the racks to start browsing. Julie couldn't help but hear their conversation as they laughed and joked with each other.

"Oh lord, Caroline, check this out, it'd be adorable on you!"

"Ha, no way in hell, Alabama. That thing is hideous."

"But it's Vera Wang!"

"Don't care, it's still butt ugly!"

The women laughed and moved on to look at more clothes. Julie held back her sigh. She missed hanging out with her girlfriends. Granted, her so-called friends back in Virginia didn't seem as close as this group of women did, but still. She'd been working so much she hadn't had time to try to meet anyone in California yet. She'd have to do something to remedy that.

Julie turned her attention to the spreadsheet on the computer in front of her, trying not to be rude and listen in on the conversation of the three women in the back of the store, but the light music couldn't drown out their happy chatter.

"Do you think Sam would like this?" One of the women asked the others.

"Uh, yeah. Are you kidding? He'll have you out of it as soon as he sees you."

They all giggled.

Finally, after an hour of browsing the store, the trio came up to the cash register to check out.

"Find everything you wanted?"

"No way, this store rocks! I wanted just about everything I saw in my size. We'll definitely be back."

Julie went into her recruitment speech as she rang up their purchases. "Well, we're constantly getting new stuff in because everything in here has been donated, so if you have any designer clothes at home that you either don't want or don't fit anymore, I'd be glad to take them off your hands. All donations are tax deductible and you'd of course get a receipt. We're also working with the local women's shelters to give free outfits to women who have interviews, but don't have the appropriate clothing to wear and can't afford to buy anything. And starting in the spring, I want to offer the same kind of service for prom dresses for the local teens who can't afford to purchase a new dress."

"Wow, really? That's awesome," one of the women exclaimed. "I don't have anything designer, that's just not me, but I bet some of the women on base might. And heck, between all of us and the guys, we could probably find people to donate."

"That would be great!" Julie gushed. "Here, take a business card. I'm willing to pick stuff up too, if that would be easier for someone. Just email or call and we'll figure it out."

"My name is Caroline. This is Alabama and Summer," the woman said, holding out her hand.

Julie shook it and said, "Good to meet you. I'm Julie."

"We haven't seen your store before, are you new?"

"Yeah, I moved here from the East Coast about a month and a half ago. I'm still getting set up, but so far I love it out here."

Summer laughed. "Yeah, what's not to love? Sun, sand, and hot sailors."

They all chuckled. Julie finished ringing up the purchases and handed the bags to the three women. "Seriously, thanks for coming in and checking the store out. I'd appreciate any word of mouth reference you can give me. I'm honestly not in this to make money, I want to help others."

Summer looked at her with a critical eye, but didn't say anything.

Julie hurried to elaborate. "I know, that made me sound like I'm bragging or doing this for publicity's sake, but it's not that, honest. I needed a change in my life. My dad is helping me finance the business, so I'm okay there, but I had a life-altering experience, and had someone help me out, so I just want to pass it on. Pay it forward. You know, karma and all that."

"Well, this seems to be a good way to do it. We wish you the best of luck. I'm sure you'll see us in here again, with our friends next time."

"Friends?"

"Yeah," Caroline chimed in. "There's six of us. We're like a girl posse or something. Our men don't get to see us dressed up all that much, but I think if we could find some kick-ass dresses we'd knock their SEAL socks off."

"SEAL?" Julie couldn't help but ask. Seems like everyone had SEALs on their minds.

"Uh-huh. We're all partnered with SEALs. It's a tough job, but someone has to do them...I mean *it*." Alabama piped up for the first time. All the women laughed and Julie waved and smiled as they left her shop.

At first Julie thought it was fate that the three women who happened to be with SEALs came into her shop just as she hung up from talking with Commander Hurt, but then she shrugged. She was smack-dab in the middle of SEAL country. It really wasn't that odd, all things considered.

The rest of the day went by fairly quickly. A few more customers wandered in and Julie tried to plan out in her head what in the heck she was going to say to the Commander when she met up with him in a few days. She had to make him understand she was a changed person. Different than she was all those months ago, when she'd met his SEALs.

She could hear in his voice that he knew all about what she'd done and the horrible things she'd said to his team and to the other woman who was rescued with her.

Julie beat down the remorse. No. She was different now. She'd make him see it, he'd hook her up with the men who saved her, and she could get on with her life. Easy-peasy.

CHAPTER 3

JULIE SAT ON THE SMALL WALL WATCHING THE WAVES crash on the shore. There was a surprisingly large amount of people milling around. Julie was a good swimmer, but hadn't made the time to check out any of the local beaches. This one was perfect. There was a lot of sand as opposed to rock, as a lot of the western coast seemed to have. It looked as though there was a slope from the beach into the water. It didn't just drop off. This allowed kids to stand at the water's edge and shriek as the waves crashed and moved up and down the coastline. There was also what looked like a large sandbar a hundred feet or so from the beach.

There were several surfers in the water. The waves weren't huge, it wasn't Hawaii after all, but some were big enough so the surfers could stand up and ride them for a little bit before they broke. Julie supposed most of the serious surfers probably got there early in the morning, at least that was what she'd always heard. She had no firsthand experience with surfers and their preferred hang-ten time.

Julie looked down at her watch. She was early. She never used to be, but now that she had to meet with people for whom time was a premium, she made it a point to always arrive about ten minutes early. It was the polite thing to do. She didn't want anyone to decide not to do business with her because she was late for a meeting.

She looked around, swinging her feet. Her toes barely brushed the sand below her. She'd kicked off her flip-flops when she'd sat down and was enjoying the afternoon sun on her legs and toes. It'd been tough to decide what she wanted to wear. Julie wanted to project a sense of sincerity and honesty, but really had no idea how to do that. She'd settled on a pair of respectable jean shorts that came down to just above her knees and a light-pink tank top. It wasn't revealing or low-cut, but seemed about perfect for the eighty-five-degree day. She would've looked stuck-up and snotty if she'd worn a business suit, and she also didn't want to look slutty.

After having a few days to contemplate about what she wanted to say, Julie wasn't any closer to figuring it out now than she was when Commander Hurt first suggested the meeting. Finally, after two more nightmares and many sleepless hours, she decided she'd wing it.

Patrick sat in his car and watched Julie. She was sitting on the containment wall around the beach area. She smiled at the antics of a couple of kids near her, and she occasionally glanced at her watch and over at the parking lot. She looked the same as the pictures he'd had Tex send over, but there was something different about her. Patrick couldn't put his finger on it. Finally, knowing he couldn't put it off anymore, he climbed out of his car and made his way to her.

He had no idea what decision he was going to make about allowing her to meet up with Cookie and the other guys, but he'd give her the benefit of the doubt for now. She'd sounded sincere on the phone, and if it was what she needed to move on from the experience, who was he to deny her?

"Hi. You must be Julie."

She looked up at him with a smile and hopped off the wall onto the sand. She smiled at him as she bent down awkwardly to grab her shoes. "Yeah," she replied and held out a hand. "Julie Lytle. Commander Hurt?"

"Patrick. Call me Patrick." He shook her hand, pleased when she gripped his tightly, then let go.

"Patrick then. It's good to meet you. Thank you for agreeing to meet with me. I appreciate it."

He shrugged. "It's the least I could do."

"Not really, but thank you just the same. So..." Her voice faded as she looked around. "Where should we—"

"How about we walk?" Patrick suggested.

"Okay."

Patrick had come prepared for walking along the sandy beach, and kicked off the worn pair of flip-flops he had on and easily stepped over the wall she'd been sitting on a moment ago.

"Wow, you're tall," she commented dryly, eyeing him up and down. He was wearing a navy-blue T-shirt that did nothing to hide his huge biceps. He might be a Commander and not go on any missions any longer, but he obviously still worked out. The cargo shorts he was wearing were knee-length and had holes on each leg, one above his left knee and another on the left thigh. They were well-worn and looked comfortable as hell. He was also wearing a pair of sunglasses. The entire package made her think of Tom Cruise in the movie *Top Gun*.

He grinned down at Julie. Now that they were both standing in the sand, Patrick could see just how tiny she was. He'd read her stats in the report from the mission in Mexico, but seeing her five-foot-two-inch frame in person was a different thing. "Six-one probably does seem tall to you, but I'm honestly not all that big compared to a lot of guys."

She shrugged. "Okay, if you say so."

They started off down the beach. Neither seemed to be in a hurry, so they took their time. Finally, Julie delved into the reason they were there. "I'm sure you read up on whatever secret files you guys keep on missions so you know what happened down in Mexico." She knew if she tried to downplay how she'd acted, it'd make her look as if she wasn't owning up to her actions. "But I'd like to explain what happened, how I got there, the real story, not the crap the media came up with...before you make your decision...if that's all right."

She watched as he simply nodded and hurried to continue before she lost her nerve.

"I was at a bar with a group of friends. Well, they weren't true friends, just people I knew. They were daughters and friends of some of the politicians my dad works with. We got together almost every weekend to let off some steam. I know, I'm honestly too old for that crap, and what 'steam' could we possibly have to 'let off,' but it was what we did. I went to the bathroom by myself, which I know is unusual for a girl."

She looked up at Patrick with a small smile, but he wasn't even looking at her. His gaze was directed at the long line of beach in front of them. She sighed and continued, deciding to cut out the extra commentary he obviously didn't care about and get to the point.

"When I came out of the bathroom, someone grabbed me from behind and stuck a needle in my arm before I could even think about screaming or struggling. He put a hand over my mouth and pulled me out the back door, which was conveniently located next to the restrooms. I was shoved into the backseat of a car and we were leaving before I'd gotten my wits about me. Then it was too late. Whatever he'd shoved into my veins was taking affect. The last thing I remember was the men speaking to each other in Spanish before I passed out.

"I have no idea how long I was out, but I woke up naked and tied hand and foot to a cot. I was thirsty and scared and I hurt. I heard more Spanish and then a man was there. On top of me. Leering down at me as he raped me. I was still confused and didn't fully understand what was happening. I lay there, disconcerted and terrified out of my brain. Finally, after three more men took their turns, they untied my wrists, threw my clothes at me, told me to get dressed and led me to a dark hut in the middle of a jungle. I had no idea what country I was in or what was going on."

Julie felt Patrick touch her lightly on the arm. "Come on, let's sit."

She looked to where Patrick was gesturing and saw a large tree, which had fallen over. They made their way over to it and Julie was thankful that Patrick gave her a hand and helped her climb up on it so she could sit. He leaned against the tree as she got settled and crossed his arms over his chest, his shoes dropped to the sand beneath them.

"If it's too painful, you don't have to continue."

"No, I want you to know why this is so important to me."

Patrick nodded and held her gaze.

Seeing no censure in his eyes, Julie took a deep breath and continued.

"So there I was, dumped in the middle of a dark hut, with no idea where I was or what was happening. The other woman, she tried to talk to me, tried to comfort me, but all I could do was cry. I wouldn't listen to anything she had to say to me. I was in denial and didn't want to hear her. I knew if she'd been there for as long as she said she had, that I was in trouble. I knew I wouldn't be able to deal with what had happened to me over and over again for another three months. So when your SEAL came in, all I wanted to do was get out of there. Anywhere was better than that damn hut, where I could be taken away and assaulted again. When he somehow sensed the other woman in the building, I was afraid taking any more time would make the bad guys find us and kill your man. Then they'd tie me down and hurt me again."

Julie wiped away the tears she hadn't realized she was shedding and continued, trying not to break down in sobs. "I begged him to go, to ignore whatever it was he heard or saw. I had tunnel vision or something and all I could think of was getting the hell out of there. I'm so ashamed of what I did. Out of everything that happened down there, that's the one thing I can't get out of my head. That if he'd listened to me, that poor woman would still be captive. She'd be..." Julie's words faded off. She couldn't even say what she knew would've become of the other woman if she'd been left.

"Thank God he didn't listen to me, though. He went to the other side of the hut, got the other girl, and we all tromped through the jungle. It's not an excuse, but I felt horrible. I hadn't eaten, I was scared, and I said unforgivably nasty things. I knew the other woman was stronger than I was. She was a good person, trying to be nice to me, letting me have more food than she should've. I knew she felt guilty because the SEAL was sent in for me and not her, and I think at the time, I felt that way too. But I swear to you, I didn't want him to get hurt."

Julie looked up at the sexy man standing next to her, not saying anything, not letting anything he was thinking show.

"When I saw him bleeding as he was hauled into the helicopter, I knew it could've been me. When they let me off, I didn't say goodbye, I didn't say thank you, I simply walked away from them and never looked back, so damn grateful to be back in my father's arms I couldn't think of anything else. It wasn't until hours later I'd started thinking about all that had happened and feeling ashamed of myself. Everyone told me how brave I'd been, and how horrible what had happened to me was, but I knew the truth."

"And what's that?" Patrick asked.

"That I was a coward. Everything I did in my life was for myself. I'd been selfish and conceited and self-centered. I didn't care about that other woman. I just wanted to get *myself* out of the situation. I didn't care about the SEAL, I just wanted out of the jungle. I didn't care about the other guys on the team, I couldn't even tell you what they looked like. I was only concerned about myself."

"I think anyone in your situation would've been the same way."

"Yeah, that's what everyone told me, but I know it's a lie."

"A lie?"

"Uh-huh," Julie said. "Because I was there. I saw that other woman. *She* wasn't like that. Her first concern was for your SEAL. She even worried about *me* and I certainly didn't deserve an ounce of her sympathy. Your SEAL wasn't like that. He was willing to give his life up for mine, even though I didn't deserve it."

"Julie, I don't think—"

"No. I'm right. But I'm trying to change. I'm really

trying. I know a lot of people see me as stuck up and a rich daddy's girl. I even moved out here with my dad's money. I wouldn't have been able to start my business without him, so in a way, I'm still being selfish. But I'm hoping that everything I'm trying to do now to help others will somehow balance out my karma a little."

Julie swallowed and hurried to finish. "I just want to do what I should've done all those months ago. A simple thank you. Tell all of them face-to-face that I appreciate what they did for me and what they do for our country. I won't take much of their time, and I know they probably don't want to hear it from me. But, I'd be more appreciative than you'd ever know if you helped me do that."

"I'll help you."

Julie let out the breath she'd been holding and felt tears well up again. She beat them back by brute force.

"On one condition."

Oh shit. "Anything," she told Patrick honestly, looking up at him, not having the first clue what his condition might be.

"Go out on a date with me."

CHAPTER 4

PATRICK HADN'T THOUGHT AHEAD OF TIME WHAT HE was going to do, but as he leaned against the tree listening to what she'd gone through at the hands of the human traffickers, and everything she was doing now to try to change her life around, he'd found himself admiring her.

It was crazy. This was *Julie*. The bitch. He'd heard from Cookie and the others what a pain in the ass she'd been. How she'd encouraged Cookie to leave the hut knowing Fiona was still there chained to the floor. How she'd complained and bitched the entire walk to the helicopter. And even how she'd walked away from all of them without a word.

The more he thought about it, the more Patrick

knew the team needed to hear from her. They needed to know everything she'd just told him, but it was her story to tell, not his.

He'd give her the chance she needed to thank the guys and he'd warn them ahead of time to give her a shot. But watching her fight to tell him her story, watching her work her way through it, made him respect her.

Patrick was a hard man. Over twenty years in the Navy, most of those as a SEAL, had made him that way. But he'd never been so moved by a story as he'd been by Julie's. It would be up to Cookie if he wanted to let Fiona meet Julie as well, so he wasn't going to let either woman know of the other's existence until the guys had met with her.

"A date?"

"Yeah. You know...dinner...maybe another walk on a beach...a date."

She looked at him in confusion for a beat. "So you can find out more about what happened down there? Why I was a bitch?"

Patrick stepped in front of her and put his hands on the rough bark of the tree at her hips, realizing he was probably overstepping his bounds after she'd just poured her heart out to him and knowing he was still practically a stranger to her. He leaned forward, trying to make sure she really heard him and saw he was serious. "No. Because despite the difference in our ages, I'm attracted to you."

"To *me*?"

Patrick chuckled and looked her in the eyes. "You."

He watched as she struggled to come to terms with what he said. When she did respond, it wasn't what he thought she'd say. "You aren't that much older than me."

He pulled back. "How old do you think I am?"

"Um..." She wrinkled her nose as she contemplated him. "Thirty-five?"

He burst out laughing. When he had himself under control, he told her, "I appreciate that, but no, I'm not thirty-five."

When he didn't say anything else, she asked, "Then how old are you?"

"I don't think I'm going to tell you."

"What? Why? I thought only women were sensitive about their ages."

"I'm not sensitive about it, but I don't want to give you any reason to say no."

The laughter died on her face and she gazed at

him for a beat. "If I say no, does that really mean that you won't help me make it right with your SEALs?"

"No. I might be a dick, but I'd never force you to go out with me. I know I said I'd set up a meeting on one condition, but I lied. I'll do it if you agree to see me again or not."

"Okay."

"Okay to the fact that I lied about the condition, or okay to going out on a date with me?"

"Both."

Patrick nodded and moved back a fraction, holding out his hand. "Come on, I'll walk you back to your car."

Julie put her hand in his and jumped off the tree. Patrick didn't let go of her and bent down to pick up their shoes. He handed hers to her and snatched up his own. He continued to hold her hand and turned them back around the way they'd come, back to the parking lot.

Julie was silent for a bit, but then said, "I don't know anything about you...other than your name is Patrick, you aren't thirty-five, and you're in charge of a Navy SEAL team."

Recognizing that she needed some reassurance, Patrick began talking. "My name is Patrick Hurt, my nickname is Hurt, for obvious reasons. I'm not thirty-five. I used to be a SEAL myself and I've been on some intense missions in my life. I like what I do now, working behind the scenes, coordinating things. I've lived here in California for what seems my entire life. My parents are both still alive, they live up north of Los Angeles. I don't have any blood brothers or sisters, but have plenty of men and women I call my family. I've never been married, I don't have any kids floating around out in the world." He paused, looking down at Julie. He waited until she looked up at him, then continued.

"I'm not impulsive. I think through everything I do before I do it. Missions, what I'm going to eat for dinner, the route I'll take home each day, how many calories I can eat based on how much I work out. Some people have called me anal."

"But..."

Patrick knew what she was going to say. It was what he wanted her to realize. "Yeah, asking you out was impulsive and out of character for me. It should tell you that this isn't a pity date. It isn't to pump you for more information. You've piqued my interest and I want to get to know you better. I like *this* Julie."

"I like her too."

"Good." They'd arrived at the parking area. "So... is next Saturday too soon?"

"Too soon?"

"For our date."

"Oh, no. Saturday's fine. What time?"

"What time are you free?"

Julie looked up, obviously trying to remember her schedule. "I have a meeting at nine in the morning with a woman who runs an after-school program for at-risk teens, then the store opens at ten. I work until four and have another meeting with a counselor from one of the high schools."

"You're a busy woman," Patrick observed as he put on his shoes.

She shrugged. "I guess. I like being busy. Keeps me from thinking too much...about stuff."

"Do you want me to pick you up, or do you want to meet me somewhere?" Patrick wanted to give her the option. It wasn't very smart to let a man pick her up at her home on a first date because if things didn't work out, the man would then know where she lived. He was completely trustworthy though, and if they didn't click on their date, he'd leave her alone, but it was ultimately her choice.

Julie bit her lip as she contemplated his question. He liked how she really thought it through before answering. "I think I should meet you somewhere.

That way if we decide to end things early, it won't be awkward if you have to drive me home."

Patrick didn't quibble. "How about if we meet at six-thirty at the new steak place that opened up near here."

"Which one?"

"The one where you pay a flat fee and get as much meat as you can eat. They bring it around to your table until you're full and tell them to stop."

"Oh, *Fogo de Chao*? That Brazilian place? I've heard of it, and people have said it's wonderful."

"That's the one."

"Okay."

"We'll play it by ear after that."

"Sounds good."

Julie turned to him. "Thanks, Patrick. Seriously. I know you didn't have to meet me today, and you didn't have to listen to me, and you certainly don't have to let me meet your guys, but it's appreciated. More than you'll know."

Patrick lifted her hand and kissed the back of it. "You're welcome. I'll see you Saturday night. Be safe out there."

"I will. See you next week."

Patrick watched as Julie walked to her nonde-script car and left the parking lot. He wondered for a beat what the hell he was doing, but when he thought about it, and it felt right, he decided to go for it. He was the type of leader who, once he made a decision, he went with it.

And he was going with it now.

CHAPTER 5

JULIE STOOD AT THE COUNTER AT *MY SISTER'S CLOSET* the following Friday afternoon, talking to her dad on the phone. He checked in frequently, and Julie knew she'd never take it for granted again.

"Hey, Daddy. How are you?"

"I'm good. How's my baby?"

Julie rolled her eyes. His baby. Whatever. "Things are great here. I had a meeting this morning with a woman who runs an after-school program for teenagers. It was an impromptu thing on my part. I have a meeting next week with another director of a different teen center, but I was passing the building on my way to work and decided to stop and see if anyone was in and would talk to me. We worked out a deal where some of the oldest girls would start volunteering at *My Sister's Closet*. In return, they'd get a clothing allowance."

"Sounds like things are going well."

"They are. I love it out here."

"I'm glad. I've been worried about you."

"I know, and I appreciate it. What's going on there? Anything new in the world of politics?"

"Actually, since you brought it up, there're rumors going around that Senator Kellogg might be making a bid for the Presidency. He wants to get the nomination and backing of the Republican Party."

"Wow, really? That's Stacey dad...right?" Julie asked incredulously. "Are you okay with that Dad?"

"Of course. What? Did you think *I* wanted to be President? No way."

Julie breathed out an exaggerated sigh of relief. "Okay, then. Good."

They both laughed.

The door chimed as a group of women entered the store. "Hey, Daddy, I gotta go. Customers."

"Okay, Princess. Stay safe out there and don't forget to call your old man once in a while."

It was a running joke between the two of them. "I will. Love you, Daddy."

"Love you too, baby. Talk to you soon."

"Bye."

"Bye."

Julie turned to the women, ready to give her welcome-to-the-store speech, and recognized three of them from the other day. "Oh, hi! It's good to see you guys again."

"Hi, Julie. Told you we'd be back! When Fiona and the others heard about this place, they had to see it for themselves!"

"Well, take your time, look around, do your worst!"

The women all laughed and dispersed around the store, checking out what had come in since the last time they were there and seeing what deals they could find.

Julie kept one eye on the group of women, making sure they didn't need any assistance with anything, as she thought about her date the next night with Patrick. She'd honestly been surprised he'd asked her out. She'd thought him extremely handsome from the second she'd laid eyes on him, but never in a million years thought he'd ask her on a date. She still thought it had something to do with the fact he felt sorry for her. But she was willing to give him the benefit of the doubt. He'd sounded sincere enough when he'd told her he wanted to get to know her better.

"Excuse me, I have a question."

Julie's thoughts were interrupted by the words spoken nearby. She immediately turned her attention to the woman standing in front of her. "Of course, what can I—"

Julie's words cut off abruptly when she looked up and saw who was standing at the counter.

"Oh my God," the woman said in a low shocked voice. "It's you."

Julie wasn't sure what to say, but didn't get a chance to say *anything*. Caroline had come up behind her friend. "What's wrong, Fiona?"

Fiona. Julie hadn't remembered the other woman's name until Caroline said it and she looked into the eyes of the woman she'd spent some of the worst days of her life with. Fiona looked a hell of a lot better than the last time she'd seen her. Healthy. She looked healthy and happy now. Julie looked down, not able to meet Fiona's eyes, and saw a wedding band and huge diamond ring on her finger. She'd gotten married. Then she remembered what Caroline had told her when she was in the store the previous week. They were all with SEALs.

Could it...? Oh lord.

"Julie, right?" Fiona asked.

Julie couldn't read her tone, but nodded and

spoke quickly, wanting to get this done before Fiona stormed out and took all her friends with her. "I'm sorry..." She trailed off uncomfortably. Could this situation be any worse?

"You know each other?" Caroline asked in confusion, looking between Fiona and Julie.

"Yes, I—" Fiona said.

"No, not really," Julie mumbled at the same time as Fiona.

Julie wanted to sink into a hole and never reappear again.

"So is it yes or no?"

The other women had converged on the counter and Julie felt decidedly ganged up on, even if that wasn't their intent.

"Julie was the woman in Mexico with me," Fiona explained softly.

The store got so quiet, the only sound was the music playing through the speakers and the occasional car passing outside.

"Oh."

Julie thought the one word out of the blonde woman, who she remembered as Summer, summed it up concisely. The disgust and scorn for the woman Julie had been back in that hot jungle came through loud and clear.

"What are you doing here?" A woman with black hair asked brusquely. "You own this store? I thought you lived out in DC?"

Julie nodded. "Yeah, I just opened last month. I moved out here. I needed a change."

"Hmm, well, I forgot I have a meeting. Sorry, we have to get going."

That time it was the brunette who'd been in with Summer and Caroline who'd spoken. The other women agreed and they all shuffled toward the door, putting the clothes they'd picked up down on a table near the cash register.

"I'm sorry!" Julie blurted again before they could leave the store, never to return. "I'm so sorry. I was a bitch. I was scared and took it out on you. There's no excuse for the things I said to you or the things I did. I was horrible and you didn't deserve any of it. I hope you're...okay...and if I live to be a hundred I'll never forgive myself for what I did out there."

Fiona didn't say anything, but her friend did. Alabama put her hands on her hips and faced Julie. "Fiona told us some of what happened while you guys were on the run in the jungle, but I'm guessing she didn't tell us everything, if your trite little apology is anything to go by." Her arms dropped and she took a step toward Julie. Caroline grabbed her arm before she could get any closer.

"Easy, Alabama."

Alabama leaned toward Julie and hissed, "You were going to *leave* her there. Who *does* that?"

When Julie didn't respond, Alabama turned on her heel and hooked Fiona's arm in hers. "Come on, Fee, let's get out of here."

Julie watched as the women filed out of the store. The perky bell tinkled as the door closed behind them, leaving an eerie silence only broken by the music playing. Julie bent her head and rested her hands on the counter in front of her, not caring that her tears splashed onto the paperwork she'd been working on before the women had entered not five minutes earlier.

"That was a disaster," Julie said to nobody. "This whole thing is a disaster. What am I doing?" She lifted her head, walked to the door, locked it, turned the sign to closed, and woodenly walked to the back of the store, away from the windows, away from the world.

She sat in one of the armchairs and curled into a ball, hugging her knees. And she sobbed.

CHAPTER 6

"I CAN'T BELIEVE SHE HAD THE NERVE TO MOVE *HERE*," Alabama groused. "I mean seriously."

"I know, and to open a store, here, where Fiona lives. I mean she treated Fiona like crap down in Mexico, why would she want to start a business here when her dad lives out in DC?"

"And she used her daddy's money to open it too. She's so spoiled."

The nasty comments continued around the table as the six women regrouped after having their world rocked that afternoon. Caroline was silent as the others continued haranguing Julie and her existence in their little corner of California. She noticed that Fiona was also quiet.

"You all right?" Caroline asked Fiona during a lull in the conversation. "That couldn't have been fun."

"I'm okay," Fiona told her friend. "I just..."

"What?" Caroline urged. She was concerned and didn't want her to have any kind of flashback, just as she'd had before. She thought Fiona was past that, but seeing Julie again could easily make her regress in her healing.

"Did she sound sincere to you?" Fiona looked Caroline in the eyes as she asked.

"Sincere? I'm not sure—"

Caroline cut Alabama off. "Yes, she did." She looked at Alabama. "I know you're protecting Fiona and that you're just as upset about this as the rest of us are, but think about things for a second. Okay?"

Alabama bit her lip and waited for Caroline to keep talking.

"We liked Julie when we were there last week, right?" When Summer and Alabama nodded, she continued. "She was funny, gracious, and super open. If asked after we left the store if we thought she was a bitch, would any of you have agreed?"

"No. I liked her. That's why we all went back today. We wanted to support her. It seemed like she was doing such a good thing with the store," Summer said softly.

"Exactly," Caroline agreed. "If what she told us is true, she's trying to help out the community. Jess, she's giving some of the dresses in there to teenagers who can't afford a prom dress." Caroline knew her words would strike a chord with Jessyka because of her work with at-risk teens.

"And you all know, because we talked about it before we went over there today, that she's also donating clothes to women's shelters to provide them with appropriate clothes to wear to interviews. I just can't reconcile *that* woman with the one who was in the jungle with Fiona." Caroline took a deep breath. "What do *you* think, Fiona?"

"I have no idea. It doesn't make sense. I was there, I heard what she said and saw what she did. She looks the same, but...not. She never met my eyes when we were in the jungle. She always looked above my head or at the ground when she spoke. She kept a tight grip on Hunter's shirt the entire time we were fleeing."

"But she wanted to leave you there, Fiona," Cheyenne said softly, having heard the entire story from Caroline one night.

"Did she?" Fiona asked, almost rhetorically.

"What do you mean?" Summer asked.

"I'm trying to remember exactly what she said when she and Hunter were about to leave and something made him turn back around one last time." Fiona paused and bit her lip, obviously trying to remember what was said back when she was being held captive.

"She was scared, like I was. She'd just been brought in, and recently had been ...uh...you know." Fiona closed her eyes as if that would help her recall Julie's exact words. "'We have to go. I want to go'."

"See? She wanted to leave you there and get out."

Fiona shook her head slowly and raised wide eyes to her friends. "No, I don't think so. Now that I think about it, I felt like she did in that hut at one point too. I would've done anything to get as far away from there as possible. But I'd become resigned. She wasn't yet. She was scared and wanted out. If I had to guess, I'd say she was only thinking about getting away from the men who'd hurt her."

"You don't think she meant to leave you, per se, but instead was focused on escaping?" Caroline tried to clarify.

"Yeah," Fiona whispered.

"But what about the rest of it?" Alabama demanded, not harshly. "You've told us how she hated the food, complained about you suffering from the effects of the drugs, and even how she didn't care if Hunter got hurt or not."

"I don't know. I wasn't in her head, so I just don't know what she was thinking. But why do I suddenly feel horrible about that entire scene back there?"

"She was crying," Caroline mentioned in a soft voice. "We were all walking out of her store and I looked back. She was standing at the register, looking off into space, and tears were running down her face."

After a moment of silence, when none of the women said anything, struggling with their own thoughts about how they now felt a little sorry for Julie, but still were pissed off for Fiona about all that had happened to her down in Mexico, Caroline stood up from her chair and went behind Fiona. She wrapped her arms around her friend's chest and put her chin on her shoulder as she hugged her. "You gonna be okay? Do we need to call Dr. Hancock so you can talk this through?"

Fiona hugged Caroline back as well as she could in their awkward embrace. "No, I'm okay. It just makes me appreciate Hunter more for his eerie sixth sense he seems to have at times, and thank my lucky stars I got out as relatively normal as I did. Yes, I still have some flashbacks, but I have all of you guys, and Hunter, and everyone else on the team. Who does Julie have?"

Everyone was silent as Fiona's words sunk in.

CHAPTER 7

PATRICK LOOKED DOWN AT HIS WATCH FOR WHAT seemed like the hundredth time that night. Seven o'clock. It looked as though he'd been stood up. Stupidly, he hadn't given his cell phone number to Julie, so she couldn't call and let him know if she was running late. Hopefully she had an emergency or something had come up, rather than her truly standing him up. After telling the hostess it looked as if he wouldn't be eating dinner after all, he got in his car and drove to Mission Valley.

He knew Julie's store was there, it was amazing the information Tex could come up with on short notice. Her store, *My Sister's Closet*, was nestled between a small bookstore and a kids' boutique that sold baby and toddler toys and clothes. The lights in the store were off, except for the security lighting, which gave off just enough light to deter any wannabe burglars.

Patrick had Julie's home address, but knew if he showed up there, he'd be a total creeper. He drummed his fingers on the steering wheel, trying to decide if he should call her or not, he'd gotten her number from Tex, finally deciding to give her some space. If Julie was having second thoughts about going on a date with him, he wouldn't push.

He didn't want to bring up any bad memories or trigger any kind of flashback. Patrick knew Fiona suffered with them and the last thing he wanted to do was make Julie more uncomfortable. He blew out a breath and murmured, "Fuck, this sucks." He pulled out onto the road and headed home. Maybe he'd get lucky and she'd call him on Monday and let him know what was going on.

———

Julie huddled on her bed, concentrating on her breathing. She'd had a hell of a nightmare, one she hadn't had in a long time. She'd halfway expected it though, maybe that's why she dreamed it tonight.

She was walking away from the hut she'd been

held captive in and she'd looked behind her as she followed the SEAL into the jungle. In her dream, he hadn't turned around. He hadn't noticed Fiona on the other side of the room. He'd left with Julie in tow and they'd abandoned Fiona back in the hut. As they fled she looked back and Julie saw Fiona sitting in the room, and there was a spotlight above her, shining down. The other woman was kneeling in a small circle of light. The chain was around her neck and she was completely naked.

Julie could see bruises all over the other woman's body and she was bleeding from several large cuts on her face, head and chest. Her hand was outstretched toward Julie and she kept saying, "Why, Why did you leave me here? You knew what would happen to me."

Julie had jerked awake, sweating and shaking. Even though she knew it wasn't what had happened, she knew it very well *could* have happened. If the SEAL hadn't been as good at his job as he was, it would have. And that ate at Julie's conscience. It was as if she had to have the dreams every now and then to remind herself who she really was. A woman who'd leave another to live a horrible existence and to most likely die a slow, painful death.

Tonight was supposed to have been her date

with Patrick, but Julie knew there was no way she could show up. After seeing Fiona and her friends at the store, it was obvious she'd never be forgiven, because what she'd done was unforgiveable. The SEALs agreeing to listen to her was a pipedream. She'd been a job to them. Nothing more, nothing less. They'd moved on; she had to as well.

So she'd stood up Patrick. He'd understand.

But Julie still felt bad. How long had he waited for her? Had he sat at the table looking at his watch, wondering if she was all right? Then when he'd finally decided she wasn't coming, was he mad? Julie bet he didn't get stood up very often. He was so good-looking. No one in their right mind would stand him up.

And that was the thing—she was obviously not in her right mind. She'd been insane to think anything she'd done to change herself and her life-style would balance out the horrible person she'd been.

Julie dug the palms of her hands into her eyes and rubbed, trying to get the horrific image of Fiona in the hut, blaming Julie for leaving her there, out of her mind. Finally, she shook her head and reached for her cell. Even though it was the middle of the night, she'd call and leave a message for Patrick. It was the polite thing to do. She hadn't grown up the daughter of a politician for nothing. As a politician, her dad might be able to be a jerk and demanding, but as his daughter if she was rude, she opened herself up to ridicule and censure by the press, and she didn't want that to blow back on her dad. Julie had to let Patrick off the hook.

She dialed the number Tex had given her, knowing Patrick wouldn't be at work and she could leave a message and could take the cowardly way out and not speak with him personally. Julie waited impatiently for the message to finish so she could talk. Finally, after the beep, she spoke quickly.

"Hi Patrick, it's Julie. Sorry I didn't show up tonight...something came up. And I've thought about it more and I won't need your help with what we talked about. It was a dumb idea anyway and selfish on my part...as usual. Thank you for your service to our country. Bye."

As far as blow-off messages went, it was pretty lame, but at least it was done.

Julie threw the phone back on the nightstand and curled up on her side, hugging her pillow. Tomorrow was a new day. She'd be fine. It was a big city. She'd never see either Patrick or Fiona and her friends again. No problem.

———

Patrick sat with three of the SEALs under his command: Cookie, Wolf, and Dude. They'd been discussing the upcoming training they'd be taking part in during the next week.

"How're things at home with Caroline, Wolf?"

"Good, although you'll never guess what happened this past weekend."

Patrick raised an eyebrow, waiting for him to continue.

"The girls ran into Julie. You know, Julie from the rescue we did down in Mexico, where Cookie found his Fee?"

Patrick looked sharply at Cookie. He was sitting back in his chair with both arms crossed over his chest, looking pissed. "Julie Lytle?"

"Uh-huh."

"And?"

"The girls were pissed. Words were spoken. Caroline said Julie tried to apologize to Fiona, but they hustled her out of the store pretty quickly."

Patrick understood why Julie had stood him up now. His heart hurt for her, but first he had to see where Cookie's head was at.

"Cookie?"

"What?"

"How's Fiona? She pissed?"

He shook his head. "You know Fee, she sees the good in everyone."

"So she wasn't upset?"

"I didn't say that. She was upset. Had a nightmare that night. We talked it through and I think she's okay now, but I'm keeping an extra eye on her. Caroline and the others are helping. But we talked about it. She feels bad for Julie."

"Bad?"

"Yeah. Julie seems to be trying really hard to make a difference in the community. She's volunteered her time and has been doing what she can to help battered and abused women and teens."

"What do you think, Cookie?"

Cookie shrugged and sat up in the chair, leaning his elbows on his knees. "I only care about Fiona. If she wants to think Julie's changed, then I'm all for it. But if she doesn't ever want to see her again, I'll do everything I can to convince Julie to move back to Virginia. I realize that makes me sound like a dick, and it's possible even if she stays, Fiona won't run into her, but I won't chance it. Fiona means the world to me and I'll do whatever it takes to make sure she's in a safe and healthy place and that she'll never suffer another flashback again...if I can help it.

Patrick thought about Cookie's words. Julie certainly had a hard road to travel to get back in his good graces, but he didn't think that was what Julie really wanted. She knew she'd never be best friends with the SEALS who rescued her. She only wanted a chance to apologize and to thank them.

Suddenly Patrick really wanted her to have that shot.

"I talked to Julie before the girls ran into her," he admitted.

"What?" Wolf questioned sharply.

"What the hell, Hurt?" Cookie exclaimed at the same time.

"Are you fucking shitting me?"

The last was from Dude, arguably the most intense of the SEALs on the team. Patrick held up his hand. "Hear me out."

When the men nodded, he continued. "Tex gave her my number. She called wanting to see if she could find out who the SEALs were who rescued her so she could thank them, and apologize."

"A day late and a dollar short," Dude grumbled.

"She knows it," Patrick confirmed. "She knows she fucked up and she wanted to make it right. I'm surprised Tex gave her my office number, but she never would've found out anything about you or how to get hold of you without Tex. Luckily he let me be the middle-man between you and her. She made a good case on the phone for wanting to apologize to you, so I went and met with her. I think she's sincere."

"It wasn't cool of her to talk to the girls," Cookie complained, knowing he was being unreasonable. It wasn't as if Julie planned for Fiona and the other women to go into her store.

"I think that was purely by chance. At no time did she mention to me about wanting to see Fiona, Cookie. She was sorry about what she did, but she didn't talk about tracking her down at all. I don't think she even knows you guys are married. Think about it, Julie owns a secondhand shop that carries high-end designer clothing. Of course your women are gonna find out about it and make their way there. It was only a matter of time before they ran into each other. And neither Julie nor Fiona are dumb. I'm sure they recognized each other immediately."

No one said anything for a moment.

"And just so we can get it all out on the table here...full disclosure and all that...I asked her out."

"You *what*? Jesus, Hurt, you can't do that!" Cookie exclaimed and stood up sharply, leaning toward his Commander with his body braced on the table with his hands.

Patrick ignored Cookie's outburst. "I can and I did, but you'll probably be happy to know she stood me up."

At his Commander's words, Cookie sat back down and ran his hand over his head. "She did?" he asked in a calmer voice.

"Yeah. We were supposed to go to dinner Saturday night."

"The girls ran into her on Friday," Cookie said solemnly.

"I know that now, I didn't then. I'm thinking after meeting them, she went over in her head whatever was said between them and she figured she might as well give up on the idea of seeing you guys."

"I think, Cookie," Wolf said carefully, "it might do you some good to meet with her. To hear what she has to say."

"I don't know, guys. You weren't there. You didn't hear how horrible she was when Fee was counting backwards to take her mind off of the fact she was going through withdrawal from the shit they'd been feeding into her veins. You weren't there when she bitched that all I had to give her to eat was granola bars. You didn't see the guilt in Fiona's eyes when she didn't think there was enough food to eat." Cookie shook his head and repeated, "I just don't know."

"Well, I think you'll have some time to think about it," Patrick told him. "I'm fairly certain I have my work cut out for me if I want to get her to agree to go out with me again."

"You really liked her that much?" Dude questioned.

"Yeah. There's just something about her. It's like she's a ten-pound terrier standing up to an eighty-pound pit bull. She's scared out of her mind, but acts like it's no big deal and that she can't be hurt by anything."

"So you feel protective of her," Dude stated. "I can understand that."

Patrick knew he could. He was very protective of Cheyenne. "Yes and no. She's been through hell and clawed her way back to the other side. She fascinates me. Many people wouldn't be as well-adjusted as she is after going through what she did. Cookie, I *know* you understand that. I figure if she can own up to what she did wrong and have the guts to try to do something about it, then I can admit that I admire her for being brave enough to go after what she feels she needs and that I want to get to know her better."

"I can't say I'm thrilled about having her around if things between you and her go well, but I'm also not that big of an asshole to say I never want to see her. I trust your judgement, Hurt; if you say you see something redeemable in her, I have to believe you. If it comes to it, and she still wants it, I'll meet with her and let her have her say."

"Appreciate that, Cookie. If I can get her to see me again, I'll see if I can make it happen."

The men stood up and Wolf clapped the Commander on the back. "Good luck, man. Women never do what you think they're going to."

CHAPTER 8

How in the hell she could have the worst luck on the planet and keep running into the seven people she least wanted to see again in her life, was beyond Julie's imagination. She knew she had a lot to atone for, but seriously, she couldn't get a break.

A week after the disastrous encounter in her store, Julie almost ran into Summer in the grocery store. She'd apologized profusely and rushed off without giving the other woman a chance to say anything.

Then on another day, Julie was driving down the road and happened to look at the car next to her at a red light, only to see Caroline sitting behind the wheel of an SUV. It seemed like Fiona's friends were everywhere.

But that wasn't the end of her torture. Julie had been visiting yet another teen center and had come face-to-face with Jessyka.

She'd somehow stumbled through some small talk and when she'd met with the director of the center, the woman had explained Jess was a frequent volunteer and a staunch supporter and friend to most of the girls who participated in the after-school programs.

Just when Julie thought she was over the worst of the accidental run-ins with the people who knew how awful of a person she could be, Patrick strode into her store as if he shopped there every day of the week.

"Hello, Julie."

"Uh, hi." She stared at him for a moment, and when he didn't say anything else, she nervously filled the silence between them. "Sorry about the other week. Did you get my message?"

"Uh-huh."

"Oh, okay. Yeah, well, something came up. I'm sorry I didn't get ahold of you. I didn't have your cell, I could only call your work number."

"Yeah, I realized that as I was waiting for you. Everything okay?"

"Yeah, thanks."

Julie fidgeted as Patrick leaned against the counter and seemingly got comfortable. It didn't look as though he was planning on going anywhere anytime soon.

"You lose my number?"

Uh-oh. "No?" The word came out more as a question than the statement Julie wanted it to be.

"Hmm. I haven't heard from you in two weeks."

"I know…I've been busy."

"Julie, I know about you running into Fiona and her friends."

Julie's head came up at that. "You do?"

"Uh-huh. I do. I also know that's why you canceled our date."

"Okay, well. Yeah, good. That *is* why. I just realized it was a stupid thing to want to talk to the guys who rescued me. I mean, it was just a job for them. They don't care, and—"

Patrick interrupted her. "How do you know they don't care?"

"Patrick," Julie said desperately, wanting the conversation to end. "They just don't. Once again, I'm being selfish. I wanted to talk to them for myself, not for them. It's just me thinking of myself again. It's fine. Seriously, can we just drop it?"

Julie couldn't meet his eye as he stood there watching her. "I'll drop it..."

She sighed in relief.

"...for now."

"Well, hell," she muttered before thinking twice about it.

Patrick chuckled. "Now that that's out the way. When are you going to let me take you out?"

"You still want to?" Julie looked up at him in disbelief.

"I still want to. And if you ask me why, I'm going to have to do something drastic."

Julie smiled for what seemed like the first time in a long time. "Well, we wouldn't want that. Okay, I'll go out with you."

"Now."

"What?"

"Now. I'm taking you out now."

"But, I'm the only one here, and I have to—"

"There's no one here. It's three. The store is only supposed to be open for another hour. Put a sign up that says you had an emergency or something."

"But I'd be lying."

Julie didn't understand the broad grin that came over Patrick's face.

"What are you smiling at?"

"You. You can't even lie about taking an hour off to do something for yourself."

When he put it that way, it sounded ridiculous. It wasn't as if she had hordes of people knocking down her door wanting to get in. "Okay, but...where are we going?"

"I thought we'd go casual today. I'd like to take you back to the beach. It's one of my favorite beaches in the area. There's good surf, good sand, and there are a couple of really good food trucks that come down to that area each night."

"Food and an evening walk on the beach. You sure do know how to treat a woman," Julie teased.

"Come on, do what you need to do before closing up. I'll wait."

Julie closed out the cash register and made a sign apologizing for the early closure and attached it to the front door of the store. "I need to run by the bank and deposit this," she told Patrick.

"You don't keep it in a safe here on site?"

Julie shook her head. "No, my dad advised against it. There are too many people desperate for even twenty bucks to risk it. I'd rather be inconvenienced and take the cash to the bank each night than to chance someone knowing I had a safe and robbing me to get at it."

"Smart."

Julie shrugged. "It was my dad's idea."

Patrick didn't say anything, but took her hand as they walked down a few businesses to the drop box at the bank. He walked them to his car and they headed off toward the beach.

Patrick lucked out and found a place to park in the first public lot he pulled into. They grabbed some burritos at a food truck that Patrick insisted were "fucking awesome," then walked along the sand, much as they had the first time they'd met, eating their dinner and talking about nothing important.

There were a lot of families enjoying the balmy evening. Kids played in the surf, floating on boogie boards, waiting for the next wave to come and propel them toward the sand. Finally, after an hour or so of walking and chatting, Patrick said he had to be getting back.

"I've got training in the morning."

"I can't picture you standing there blowing a whistle, yelling at grown men to run faster," Julie teased.

"That's because I don't stand there. I'm right there running with them."

"You are?"

"Yeah. I am."

"I figured you worked out, because you're definitely in shape, but I didn't think you worked out with the SEALs."

Patrick chuckled. "And why not? Because I'm old?"

"Oh lord, no," Julie said and blushed. "I didn't mean it like that. And I still have no idea how old you really are. Fifty-three?"

"Ouch, woman. I think I liked your other guess of thirty-five better. And how *did* you mean it, if you didn't mean I was old?"

She put her face in her hands and shook her head. "Never mind. So...you have training in the morning?"

Patrick laughed and pulled her hands away from her face. "You're so cute. And yes. Around o-four-hundred in the morning. We're meeting on the beach to run through some exercises with the SEAL wannabes."

Julie caught the evil look in his eye. "And you love torturing them, don't you?"

"Of course."

"Well, come on then. Can't have Cinderella changing into a pumpkin before she has to get home from the ball."

They walked back to the parking lot and Patrick opened the passenger-side door for her and patiently waited until she was settled to close it. He drove them back to her store and when he pulled up to her car, he said, "Wait here."

Julie watched as he got out and surveyed the area carefully, before coming around to her side and opening her door. He helped her out and at her curious look, simply said, "Just making sure it was safe."

Goosebumps rose on Julie's arms at his words. *Just making sure it was safe.* Six words that were quite possibly the most romantic thing she'd ever heard. He was either really good at knowing what to say, or he was the real deal. Julie wasn't sure yet.

She clicked the locks on her door and stood in the open driver's side. "Thanks for dinner, and for the nice night."

"You're welcome. And before I forget, here's my contact numbers. Now you don't have an excuse not to call me again."

Julie took the business card Patrick held out to her. He'd written his cell phone number on the bottom, along with another number that she recognized as being from Virginia. She raised her eyebrows at him.

"It's Tex's number."

"Ah, the mysterious Tex again," Julie said in confusion.

"Yeah. If you ever need anything and can't get ahold of me, you can call Tex. He'll find me."

"I'm not going to call Tex. I don't know him."

"It doesn't matter if you know him or not. There's no one I trust more than him. And if you need me, and can't get ahold of me, he will most definitely be able to get me to you."

Julie shook her head in exasperation and barely resisted rolling her eyes, instinctively knowing Patrick wouldn't appreciate it. "Yeah, okay. Have fun at training in the morning."

"You gonna give me your number?"

"Oh, yeah." Julie rattled off the numbers to him. When he didn't move to write them down, she asked him about it.

"I've got it. I don't need to write it down."

"Prove it," she challenged.

"What do I get if I'm right?"

"What do you want?"

"A kiss."

Julie was surprised, but not upset. "Okay. A kiss."

Patrick recited her number back seemingly without even thinking about it. Before the last number had left his lips, he'd taken a step toward her, crowding her against the frame of her car. He put both hands around the sides of her head and rested his thumbs on her jawbone. Julie grabbed hold of his wrists and looked up.

"I'm going to kiss you now, Julie."

"Okay," she whispered in agreement.

His lips came down on hers and Julie went up on tiptoe to try to get closer to him. She didn't think to let go of his wrists and wrap her arms around him, because she was too busy trying to memorize the feel of his lips on hers.

Patrick ran his tongue along the seam of Julie's mouth, as if he was asking permission to enter. She opened gratefully and sighed when Patrick's tongue swept inside. It felt as if he was branding her. He was hard where she was soft. He was tall to her short. He was über masculine to her feminine frame.

Unfortunately, Patrick didn't linger long. The kiss wasn't passionate, but completely appropriate for a good-night kiss after a first date. He lifted his head from hers, but didn't move his hands. He gazed down at her for a long moment before saying, "I liked that."

Julie smiled. "Me too."

"Okay then. I'll call you."

"Good."

Finally, he dropped his hands, forcing her to let go of him, and he turned her gently toward the car. "In you go. I'll talk to you soon."

Julie sat and started the engine. Seeing he was still standing there watching her, she rolled her window down and told him, "I had a good time tonight. Thanks."

"You're welcome. Drive safe."

"You too." Feeling proud that she only looked back once, Julie smiled all the way to her small apartment.

CHAPTER 9

Julie sat in the circle of Patrick's arms on his couch as they watched *World War Z*. They'd spent time together almost every day since their first "date" a month ago. As far as their physical relationship went, they were taking it slowly, which was fine with Julie.

Yes, she'd had a horrible experience when she'd been kidnapped, but she'd mostly dealt with it. Her dad had immediately gotten her into therapy. She'd also seen a couple of doctors and found out she'd been incredibly lucky and hadn't picked up any diseases from her experience, thank God for something going her way after the hell she'd been through. All in all, Julie knew it could've been a hell of a lot worse, and she chose to focus on the positives rather than losing herself in the negatives of the entire experience.

Dealing with the physical aspects of having a boyfriend, Julie was realizing, was actually much easier than the mental ones. She thought it'd be easy to open up to Patrick and let him know how she was feeling about herself, and about the nightmares she continued to have, especially after their first walk on the beach when she'd tried to explain how important it was to her to be able to thank the SEALs who had rescued her.

But after the cold reception she'd received from Fiona and her friends, and realizing that saying "sorry" wasn't going to suddenly make her feel better about the person she used to be, the urge to open up to Patrick had waned. Hell, it hadn't just waned, it had disappeared altogether.

Julie knew Patrick was trying to ease her into a physical relationship, and she appreciated it. As much as she might have projected a party-girl image back home, she'd never been the type of girl to fall into bed with men on the first date...or even the second or third. She liked to be friends with someone before getting naked with them.

She was certainly ready to get physical with Patrick

though. She liked him. He was funny, good-looking, and seemed sincerely interested in her. She'd even told him last week she was ready, but he'd only kissed her on the forehead as if she was twelve, and said *she* might be, but *he* wasn't. Julie would've thought it was a blow off if he hadn't kissed the hell out of her, almost brought her to orgasm with his mouth on her nipples, and if she hadn't seen him every day since then.

Patrick leaned over and muted the television. Julie watched as the zombies silently began to swarm over the wall built around Israel on the screen. She had a feeling whatever Patrick had been wanting to talk to her about before moving them to the next level, now was the time.

"I know you told me you didn't care anymore, but I spoke with the SEALs who rescued you, and they're willing to meet with you."

Julie froze. Oh God. She'd known this would be coming sooner or later. She tried to play it off. "It's okay. I've changed my mind. I've made peace with it." Which was a total lie, but she didn't want to have to deal with their rejection of her apology and thanks as she had with Fiona.

Patrick turned Julie in his arms and pulled her over his lap until she was straddling him and he could look her in the eye, her arms wrapped around his neck.

"Julie. I think you need this. I heard what you told me that first day on the beach."

"Really, Patrick, I'm good. I just needed—"

"You're not good."

"I am," Julie insisted, not very convincingly, even to her own ears.

"You fell asleep on the couch over here last week." Patrick's words were low and earnest. "The second you were down, you started dreaming. I watched you do it. You whimpered in your sleep and called out 'I'm sorry,' over and over. You only stopped when I sat next to you and took you in my arms. You never even woke up until later, when I purposely shook you awake so I could take you home."

Julie stared at Patrick in dismay.

"It's eating you up inside. You need this."

She looked down, sucked her bottom lip into her mouth and stayed silent, not knowing what to say.

"What's holding you back?"

Julie didn't want to tell him, but he was a good guy. He'd been nothing but decent. He'd encouraged her when she doubted both herself and what she was doing with the store, he supported her, he laughed with her, he was a good kisser, and he never, not once, made her feel like the bitch she'd been in what seemed like a previous life.

Most importantly, Julie liked Patrick. If she wanted any kind of real relationship with him, she knew they had to get past this. He was the SEALs' Commander, for Christ's sake. She'd have to see them sooner or later if she and Patrick stayed together. It was a miracle they hadn't already, but she knew that was probably all Patrick's doing.

"What if they don't accept my apology?"

"They will," Patrick said immediately, knowing exactly who she was talking about.

"Fiona didn't," she admitted in a small voice. "Why would they?"

"What do you mean, Fiona didn't?" Patrick asked with concern. He put his finger under her chin and lifted her head. "I know you saw her that one time, and I know there was some shit said."

Patrick had talked to the guys about the incident, and while he knew it wasn't a sunshine-and-roses meeting, he hadn't been aware any of the girls had said anything over-the-top mean. He didn't think it was in them, not after everything they'd been through.

Julie shook her head, lying. "Not really. Look, I

don't blame her friends. I was mean to Fiona in the jungle, and she and her friends have the right to not want to talk to me."

"Julie, I talked to the guys. I don't think you know this, you might suspect it, but Fiona is married to the SEAL who got you through the forest. I talked to him. Cookie knows you saw Fee and that you apologized. He would've told me if she was still harboring ill will toward you."

"I figured they were married," Julie said softly, feeling the pit in her stomach grow bigger and bigger, "But I guess I didn't realize it until I saw her that she was married to the SEAL that saved us."

"Yeah," Patrick confirmed.

"I'm not talking to him, or any of the others," Julie stated resolutely.

"Julie, you—"

"No!" She struggled to get off Patrick's lap, relieved when he let her go. "I can't. She was upset to see me. I know her husband has to be pissed at me." Julie paced as she continued. "I can't face him. I thought I could...before. But knowing they got together? That they bonded so completely while we were in that fucking jungle that they fell in love and got married?" She spared a glance at Patrick, not knowing how to put into words what she was thinking.

Julie didn't *really* think if she'd been less of a bitch, *she* might have ended up with the handsome SEAL instead of Fiona, but the thought wouldn't leave her brain. "I'm assuming that's what happened, right?" she finished somewhat lamely.

"Basically, yeah."

"Yeah. So I'm not doing it."

"They're my men," Patrick said in a low, sad voice. "I want you to be there when we have company picnics. I want you to be a part of my Navy life. If you won't see them, you can't be."

Julie felt her heart breaking. She was losing one of the best things to happen to her before she'd even truly had it. But she really was a coward. She couldn't face Fiona again. Couldn't face the censure she saw in all of her friends' faces. Could *not* face the man who loved Fiona, who'd been there in Mexico to see her at her worst. She couldn't do it.

"I can't."

"I'll take you home then. Give you some time to think about it. We'll talk later."

Julie nodded, numb inside. She never should have come to California. She hadn't known at the time this was where the SEALs were stationed who had rescued her, but she should've remembered the Naval base nearby was the home of the SEALs and it was a likely possibility.

Patrick helped her with her coat and led her outside to his car. He opened her door as he always did and waited until she was comfortable before shutting it. He got in without a word and they drove to her apartment in silence.

He pulled into a visitor's parking space and turned to her. "I like you, Julie. I want to be with you. I'm forty-three years old." He watched as she turned to stare at him in disbelief. "I know, I've never told you my age, but there it is. I'm old enough to know what I want in a partner. I've never been married for a reason, because I've never found someone who I can imagine being with for the rest of my life...until you. I know there's a fifteen-year age difference between us, but I don't care."

"Patrick..." Julie started, having no idea what she was going to say, but she didn't have to think of anything, because he continued.

"I know you have demons, we all do. You think after spending most of my time in the Navy as a SEAL, I don't? I've seen some of the worst things you can imagine, and even some you can't. But you have to fight your demons, otherwise they'll take control

of you. And sweetheart, they're taking you over. I've
seen it the last month or so. When you first called
me I didn't want to meet you, but you wouldn't take
no for an answer. You were so sure about what you
needed to do to move on. But at the first sign of
adversity, you gave up. And I know that isn't you."

"It *is* me. You weren't there, you didn't—"

"I wasn't there," Patrick interrupted without a
qualm, "but I've been in similar situations. I've gone
into various countries and rescued kidnap victims.
Some were easygoing, some were scared, some were
combative and hostile. I've *seen* it. But, Julie, you told
me yourself that you were a different person now
than you were then. I *like* the Julie that's sitting in
front of me right now. Is everyone in this world going
to like you and want to be your best friend? No. I
have enemies. I can be a real hard ass and there are
SEALs all over this country that I know wouldn't
mourn me if they learned I'd suddenly passed away.
But Julie, that's *their* issue, not mine.

"I have friends, good friends. I'm happy with my
life. If I could do it all again, would I do everything
the same? Of course not, but that's a part of life.
Learning from your mistakes and moving on. I want
you to move on with me. But if that's going to
happen, you're going to have to do what you came

out here to do—apologize and thank my men. Whatever they do with that is on *them*, not you."

"But they're your men."

"They are. And I know them. You think I'd be giving you this advice if I thought they'd hurt you? No way in hell. But you have to trust me, and them. More importantly, you have to do what *you* need to in order to move on. And God, Julie, I want you to be able to move on with me. I'd like nothing more than instead of waking you up and taking you home, to wake you up with kisses and carry you into our bedroom, where I could make sure you'd sleep like a log every night. I want nothing more than to learn your sweet little body inside and out, to taste you, to hear what you sound like when I'm buried deep inside you—but I can't until I know you're with me. Until I know this can go somewhere."

"Patrick," Julie almost moaned.

"I know I'm not playing fair, but I need to lay it on the line. I like you. I want you. But you need to forgive yourself, and then let my men forgive you. There's a company picnic at La Jolla this weekend. They're usually over at Coronado, but everyone wanted a change. I'd love to get the apology out of the way beforehand, so you can join me there and we can move on, together."

He waited a beat, then said in a low, urgent voice, "I have a feeling you're it for me, Julie. I know we didn't meet under normal circumstances, but I thank God every day that you knew someone who knew a Navy SEAL there in Virginia. I'd say it's amazing he knew Tex, but Tex knows everyone. Tex is a very important part of my men's lives, and has had a hand in saving every single one of their women. He wouldn't have given you my number if he thought what you wanted to do would hurt Cookie or Fiona or any of the other men and the women they love. Please, sweetheart. Be there on Saturday. Let's do this so we can start the rest of our life together."

He stared at Julie for a moment, then turned and climbed out of the driver's seat. He held her open door for her after she got out, leaned down and kissed her on the forehead. There was no making out, no getting to second base and thinking about stealing third.

"Sleep well, and I mean that, Julie. Hopefully I'll see you in a couple of days." Patrick squeezed her shoulders once and then he was done.

Julie headed to her apartment in a trance. Every single word Patrick said was seared on her brain.

He was right. She knew he was, but she under-stood if she showed up to talk to his men on Saturday, it'd be one of the most difficult things she'd ever done in her life, and she wasn't sure she had it in her, not even for Patrick. Not only would she be opening herself up to his men, and possibly have them treat her with indifference at best and censure at worst, but she'd be letting Patrick know in no uncertain terms that she wanted to be with him too.

She honestly didn't know if she could do it.

CHAPTER 10

THE NEXT DAY, JULIE PULLED HERSELF OUT OF BED, knowing she wouldn't be able to sleep any more than the three hours she'd somehow snuck in between nightmares. She put on her bathing suit and a pair of shorts and a T-shirt. She threw on a pair of pink flip-flops and grabbed sunscreen, a towel and her phone. She jumped in her car and went to *My Sister's Closet* and put up a "closed for sickness" sign for the first time since she'd moved to California. She needed a day to herself to think about what she wanted to do with her life.

That done, she headed for the beach. She'd always loved swimming, and was actually very good at it. Back in Virginia, she'd gone to the pool and done laps for exercise almost every day. She was in southern California, she needed sun and sand. That was supposed to cure all ailments.

Julie parked at the popular La Jolla beach, knowing she chose it partly because it was the beach she met Patrick at, and walked toward a section where a lot of others were sunbathing and hanging out. She didn't want to be alone and being in the middle of families and others enjoying their day at the beach seemed like a place she wanted to be.

She spread her towel on the sand and stripped off her clothes. She lay back on the sand and tried to relax. Julie closed her eyes and ran through different scenarios in her head. She thought back to the scene in her shop with Fiona and her friends. If she was honest with herself, she didn't blame any of them for acting as they did.

She'd been blindsided with coming face-to-face with Fiona, but if *she'd* been treated as badly as Fiona had been, and then come face-to-face with her tormenter, Julie knew she would've acted the same way Fiona and her friends had. And to be fair, Fiona hadn't thrown her apology back into her face, she just kind of looked at her, shell-shocked.

Julie wondered for the first time since that horrific day if maybe, just maybe if she tried again, she could get Fiona to listen to her. She knew they'd probably never be best friends, and that was okay. But if Julie wanted to be with Patrick, *really* with him, they'd see each other every now and then.

Julie didn't know if the Commander hung out with the SEALs or not; she figured maybe not on a social basis. If he had to send them on dangerous missions and make decisions that affected their lives, he was probably more of a professional friend than a personal one. However, he had hinted that the SEALs were like family to him. She could probably handle seeing Fiona and her friends every now and then, especially if she didn't have to worry about fitting into what was obviously their close circle, but she wasn't sure about having to see them and hang out with them on a social basis. It'd probably be too painful for Fiona, and would definitely be awkward for Julie.

Then there were the SEALs themselves. She definitely hadn't put her best foot forward with them, but men were typically better at not holding grudges and moving on. Fiona's husband notwithstanding, maybe the others would be able to forgive her for being a bitch. She'd have to work harder to show Cookie she'd changed, and wasn't that horrible person he'd had to deal with in the jungle, but maybe she could do it.

Julie was aware that sometime between last night and today her attitude had shifted, but she'd thought long and hard about what Patrick had said the night before. She'd come to the conclusion that he was right. And more than that, she wanted to be with him too. And if that meant she had to put on her big girl panties and apologize and take whatever the SEALs wanted to dish out to her, she'd do it. Patrick was that important to her. How that had happened so quickly, Julie had no idea, but it had.

And besides, she needed to move on with her life, it's why she'd moved out to California in the first place. The nightmares had increased since she'd seen Fiona, and it was obvious she needed closure. Whether or not any of them forgave her was almost secondary at that point. She'd do the best she could, and that would have to be good enough for her psyche.

Julie was feeling mellow, enjoying the warmth of the sun and the breeze off the water and satisfied with her plans for her future, when she heard the first shout. She ignored it, figuring it was kids goofing off in the surf.

When more shouts came, they sounded more panicked than the first. Julie sat up and opened her eyes, shielding them from the sun with one hand.

There were about twenty teenagers in the water, yelling and frantically waving their hands, yelling for help.

Julie looked around. There were three lifeguards running toward the ocean. She knew there was no way the three of them would be able to help all of the people in the water. They needed more help.

Julie reached for her phone almost without thinking. She swiped it to open it and pushed the contact button. She pushed Patrick's name and watched the horror unfolding in front of her with a sinking feeling in her stomach.

The kids were caught in a massive rip current. They were quickly being swept farther and farther out to sea. Julie had learned all about rip currents last year before she'd been kidnapped. She'd taken a trip to Florida with some friends and had seen a small one down there. The lifeguard quickly leaped into action and had made sure the man caught in it made it back to shore. He'd then held an impromptu lesson on rip currents with the awestruck crowd; what caused them and, most importantly, what to do if you were ever caught in one.

And what you should never do was what the kids in the water were now doing. They were panicking and trying to swim directly back to shore. There was no way they were strong enough to fight the current and get back to the shallow water. The only thing they were doing was exhausting themselves and making the likelihood of drowning more like a probability.

Finally, when Julie didn't think Patrick was going to pick up and she'd have to call the mysterious Tex, she heard, "Commander Hurt here."

"Oh thank God! Patrick, it's Julie."

"What's wrong?"

She was thankful he got right down to it. "I'm at La Jolla beach and there's a rip current. A big one. There are about twenty kids caught in it and only three lifeguards. I don't know what you can do all the way from down there, but I thought maybe—"

"I'm on it. Stay out of the water. You hear me?"

"Uh huh, hurry Patrick. It's not looking good."

"I will. I'll talk to you later."

"Bye." Julie hung up the phone and stood, fidgeting from foot to foot. She chewed her nail, hoping to God she wouldn't have to watch the kids disappear forever. Their heads were getting smaller and smaller as they were swept farther and farther out to sea.

"Johnnie!"

Julie turned at the sharp cry. A woman was

rushing to the water trying frantically to grab her child, who'd wandered out just a bit too far. Julie wanted to rail at the mother for not watching her child more carefully. Who let their kid get in the ocean when it was obvious what was happening?

Acting without thinking, Julie dropped her cell phone on her towel and ran toward the little boy. Maybe she could get to him before he got sucked out into the ocean. She ran past the hysterical woman, yelling at her, "I'll get him!" before diving into the water and swimming as hard as she could toward the panicking little boy.

Blocking out her own fear, not thinking about the danger she was putting herself in, Julie stroked hard through the water. Before long, she could feel herself being dragged along with the rip current. It actually helped propel her faster toward the child. He was bobbing up and down in the water, clearly panicking. The small waves were washing over his head every now and then and he'd inhale sea water. She finally got near enough that she could grab hold of his flailing arm. As most drowning people do, he latched onto her neck with both arms and tried to climb upward, toward the precious oxygen his body was craving, almost pulling her under in the process.

Julie tucked her head as she'd been taught in a

lifeguarding class a long time ago and ducked under the water, making sure to keep hold of the boy. He immediately let go in order to stay near the surface of the water and Julie was able to turn him until his back was to her. She crawled back up his body until her head broke the surface. She put one arm around him and pulled him into her, holding him to her chest as she treaded water with her legs and her free arm.

"I've got you, you're okay. Relax. Don't fight me. Stop struggling." Finally, her words seemed to sink in, and the boy calmed. He still held onto the arm that was around his chest with both hands, his little fingernails digging in, but he'd stopped thrashing. Julie ignored the pain of her arms, and scrutinized her surroundings for the first time since she'd entered the water.

Her heart sank; they were way far away from the shore.

Resolutely, she looked around. Julie knew the best way to get out of a rip current was to swim parallel to the shoreline. Eventually they would break free of the strong current trying to carry them out to sea, but she had no idea how far she'd have to swim, or how far they'd be washed out before they were able to separate themselves from the grip of the water.

Julie wasn't thinking about herself, or her dad, or her situation with Fiona and the SEALs, not even thinking about the horrible things that had happened to her when she was kidnapped. She was wholly focused on the little boy in her arms and getting them both back to the beach.

"What's your name?" she asked him. She knew it was Johnnie, but wanted to keep him engaged with her, rather than on what was happening around him.

"J-J-Johnnie."

"Mine is Julie. Hey, both our names start with the letter J. Cool right?"

"Yeah," Johnnie said uncertainly.

"How old are you?"

"Five."

"Five? You're probably in kindergarten aren't you?"

"Uh-huh."

"Have you ever taken swimming lessons?"

"Yeah." He perked up for the first time since Julie started talking with him. "I'm a good swimmer. Even my teacher says so."

"So you know how to float?"

"Floating's for babies."

Julie couldn't help but smile. "Okay then, here's what we're gonna do. I'm going to let go and—"

"Don't let go!" Johnnie screamed and dug his nails into her arm again, harder this time.

"Johnnie, listen! I'm not going to let you get away from me. I'm only going to take my arm from around your chest so you can lie on your back. I need you to float on your back for me. I'm not going to leave you out here. Okay?"

"Promise?" His voice was wobbly and Julie could tell he was on the verge of tears.

"I promise, Johnnie. You can touch me the entire time. Okay?"

"Okay. Just don't let go."

"I won't. Now, release my arm and lay back. I'm still right here with you." Relieved when he did as she asked and tentatively put his head back until he was looking up at the sky. Julie kicked harder and put both hands under him, one at his shoulder blades and the other at the small of his back. She knew she couldn't tread water next to him like this forever, but she needed to get him comfortable first. Julie tried to strategize her next course of action. Johnnie's little body was rigid and he wasn't exactly floating, but Julie figured she could work with it.

"Good job. You're a very good floater, Johnnie. I'm proud of you. Now, I need one of the hands that's under your back to help me swim, so you'll only feel one of them, but I'm right here, I won't let you out of my grasp."

"Okay, Julie. I trust you."

Julie breathed a sigh of relief. Thank God, she needed a hand to help her swim. She kicked her legs and took an experimental stroke with her arm. So far so good. She was moving sideways. She had no idea how long it would take for them to get out of the rip current, but any progress sideways rather than out to the vast never-ending ocean was good.

Slowly but surely, Julie moved them sideways, watching as the shore got smaller and smaller. Dear God, she had no idea rip currents could go on for so long. She thought once they got a certain distance away from the shore, they simply stopped. She'd obviously been wrong.

Just when she thought they'd never break free of the grip the ocean seemed to have on them, Julie felt the tension of the water decrease. She kept kicking and pulling with her arm until she was sure she was no longer pulling against the strong current. Thank God.

"Guess what, Johnnie?"

"What?"

"We're going to start back in for the beach again. That sound okay to you?"

"Uh-huh. I want my mommy."

"I know, and you're being very brave."

Julie realized that for the moment she wasn't scared at all. It was amazing how, when you were trying to save someone else, you weren't afraid for yourself. She vaguely wondered if that was how it was for the SEALs when they were on a mission.

Another thought struck her. As scared as Johnnie was, and he'd hurt her when he'd been scared, it didn't matter to her. She was going to do the best she could for him anyway.

It was an epiphany, but she didn't have time to dwell on it.

"Do you want to try treading water for a moment, Johnnie?" Julie needed a break. She had a long way to swim back to shore and as much as she wanted to get to it, she knew if she didn't rest for a second, she'd be in trouble.

She helped Johnnie upright and kept her hand on his elbow as she scissor-kicked her legs.

"I'm tired."

"I know you are, baby, and we're gonna get you back as soon as possible."

"But I wanna be back nooooow," Johnnie complained petulantly.

Julie figured rest time was over. It hadn't been long enough, but the little boy was obviously too scared and tired to handle treading water for long.

"Okay, Johnnie. Lie back down and kick your legs, I'll get us back to shore lickety-split."

The little boy continued to complain while Julie towed him next to her and slowly made her way back to safety.

"Are we there yet? I want my mommy!" Julie felt helpless as the tears fell down his little face and disappeared into the blue water of the ocean.

She picked up her head at the sound of a motor in the distance. Thank God! The Calvary had arrived! There were four boats headed her way. They were flying across the water. If they'd been on dry land, they surely would've been breaking the law with how fast they were going. At the moment, however, Julie knew she'd never seen a better sight.

Julie turned to estimate where she'd escaped the rip current and was surprised to see heads bobbing quite a distance away from her. The boats zoomed past her and Johnnie's location and toward the teenagers who'd originally gotten swept away.

"Why'd they go past us? Are we gonna die? I

want my mommy!" Johnnie cried. Julie saw he'd turned his head and was watching as the rescue boats raced into the distance.

"They'll be back for us. There are people worse off than us. People who can't float as well as you can, buddy. Just stay floating, they'll be back."

Julie hoped like hell she wasn't lying. The beach looked a long way away and she knew her strength was flagging. She honestly didn't know if she'd be able to get them both all the way back to the shore.

CHAPTER 11

PATRICK KEPT HIS EYES GLUED TO THE WATER IN FRONT of them as Cookie raced through the waves. As soon as he'd hung up with Julie, he'd mobilized his crew. They had all happened to be down at the SEAL training beach, showing some of the recruits some maneuvers.

Patrick had raced to them, barking orders as he ran. "This is not a drill! Rip current at La Jolla beach. At least twenty people caught."

The team was moving before he'd finished speaking. Patrick was the only one not wearing the proper gear, but no one said a word. His battle dress uniform, blue and gray camouflage, was appropriate for everyday wear in the office, but on a mission on the ocean, not so much. Not caring, he leaped into a boat with Cookie and Wolf and the others got into the other two boats. Two other instructors on the beach jumped into the last boat and they were all on their way without knowing exactly what the situation was, only that if the Commander came racing down the beach yelling about a rip current, it was serious.

Patrick filled Cookie and Wolf in on what he knew as they raced across the water, their legs bending with the movement of the boat and the waves as if second nature.

"How'd you find out so quickly?" Wolf questioned.

"Julie called me. She was there as it happened."

"Smart of her," Wolf complimented.

They arrived at La Jolla beach and could see a couple of the lifeguards on jet skis in the general area where they needed to go, towing some of the teenagers back to shore.

The SEAL team immediately began to assist, pulling as many people into the boats as they could find. The surfers were all scared and mildly dehydrated from swallowing the salty water and being out in the sun for as long as they'd been, but generally all right. They'd been lucky.

Wolf, Cookie, and Hurt were the first back to

shore with their boatload of rescued swimmers. They were greeted by a huge crowd of worried, scared, and curious onlookers. As the kids exited the SEAL boat, a panicked voice rung out over the other general chaos surrounding them.

"Where's my baby? Did you find him?"

Thinking the lady shrieking at them was looking for her teenager, Cookie tried to calm her down. "The other boats are picking up the others. I'm sure he'll be here soon."

"But he's just a baby. He can swim, but not that well. He's only five!"

"Five?" Patrick questioned sharply.

"Yes! I was watching what was happening and didn't realize he'd gone into the water. He's always been curious about the lifeguards and he's been going to swimming lessons. He must've either wanted a closer look or he thought he could help in some way. The current took him away from me before I could get to him. A lady ran in after him, but I haven't seen her come in on any of the boats yet either. You have to find him! He's my only child! Please!"

Patrick looked around uneasily and didn't see Julie anywhere. "A woman went after him? Who?"

"I don't know who, she just told me to stay put

and she'd get him for me."

Patrick turned to his men. "I have a bad feeling about this."

Wolf didn't say a word, but after helping the last swimmer out, immediately climbed back into the boat, with Patrick following along behind him. Cookie pushed the inflatable raft with the powerful engine backwards until it had enough depth to turn around, then he leaped inside. Wolf took off, headed back out to sea.

Patrick and Cookie scanned the ocean surface with their binoculars. They didn't see anyone else in the area where all the surfers and boogie boarders had been located.

"Widen the search," Patrick ordered. "I don't know what she knows about rips, but if she knew anything at all, she'd try to swim parallel to get out of it. It has to be why they weren't in the general area with the others. They could be anywhere either right or left of the main current area."

Nobody wanted to mention the possibility that she, and the missing little boy, could have drowned, but each of the men were thinking it.

Wolf cut the engine and grabbed a pair of binoculars. Cookie looked to the right, and Wolf and Patrick looked left. They scanned the surface of the ocean for anything that might look out of place. Spotting a person's head bobbing in the waves was almost impossible. They all knew it, but none of them said a word.

Finally, Wolf said calmly, "I might have something." Cookie immediately dropped his binoculars and grabbed hold of the wheel, turning it to the left and heading to the area Wolf and Patrick had been scanning.

"Turn to your eleven o'clock," Wolf ordered Cookie. "Yeah, right there. Straight ahead, we'll run right into whatever it was I saw."

Patrick dropped the binoculars he'd been squinting into, preferring to see with his own eyes whatever it was Wolf had spotted and praying it was Julie.

The boat slowly made its way to the dark spot in the ocean. As they got closer and closer, they could all make out a dark-haired head bobbing up and down. Then an arm raised and waved at them.

Thank God.

———

"Hey Johnnie, look!" Julie said excitedly. "A boat!"

"A boat? Where?" Johnnie asked, immediately

sitting up in his excitement. Julie sucked in a mouthful of sea water as she struggled to keep the boy's head above the surface.

"Move your legs, Johnnie," she begged. "Tread water."

"I'm too tired," he whined, clinging to Julie's neck.

Julie's legs moved faster to keep both of their heads above water. She was holding Johnnie like she would if they were standing on firm ground. She had her hand under his bottom and he had both legs wrapped around her waist and both arms around her neck. Julie used her free hand to try to help keep them afloat.

Thinking back to Johnnie's complaint, Julie agreed. She was also tired. Exhausted, but she could hang on for another minute or so until the boat reached them. It would suck to be so close to rescue to fail the little boy now.

Finally, after what seemed like hours but was only seconds, the boat was there.

It looked so much bigger now that it was right next to her than it did from far away. Earlier, she'd watched as the boat headed away from the shore and had stopped dead in the water. She'd wondered what they were doing, but hoped they were scanning the area for more people. She'd waved her hand over her head, praying they'd see her. She'd breathed a sigh of relief when it seemed they had.

Julie looked up and was shocked to see Patrick's face peering down at her and Johnnie.

"Hi."

If she had the energy and the free hand to smack herself in the forehead, she would've. "Hi?" That's what she said to the man she thought she wanted to spend the rest of her life with after he kind of broke up with her and after she'd just spent what seemed like an hour treading water in the ocean not knowing if she'd ever put her feet on dry land again? Good lord, she was a dork.

"What's his name?" Patrick was all business.

"Johnnie."

"Hi, Johnnie. I'm Hurt. The guys with me are Cookie and Wolf. How about getting out of the ocean, huh?"

"I want my mommy."

"I know, buddy. And we'll get you to her in just a minute. Can you lift your arms so we can help you in the boat?"

"No! Don't wanna let go of Julie."

Julie turned her attention away from Patrick and Cookie. Shit. It *had* to be Cookie, didn't it? It looked as if she was going to have to face him sooner rather than later. The choice had just been taken out of her hands. But first things first.

"Johnnie, it's okay. I won't let go until you're safe in the boat. Okay? You've been such a brave boy this entire time. But let Cookie and Hurt help now. Yeah? They're Navy SEALs...the best of the best. They're almost like superheroes. They aren't going to let anything bad happen to us."

"Promise?"

Julie smiled at Johnnie. "Promise."

Even though she'd promised, Johnnie still was reluctant to let go of what he obviously knew was the only thing keeping him alive. Finally, he lifted his arms up just enough for Wolf to grab both of his wrists and easily lift him up and out of the water and into the boat. Julie breathed a sigh of relief. Even though the boy hadn't been terribly heavy, she was exhausted and the burden of knowing he was relying on her to keep him alive had been a heavy one. She looked up at Patrick.

"Your turn, Julie. Lift your arms."

She treaded water and looked at the boat dubiously. It was a rubber raft, the kind she saw on documentaries about SEAL training. There was no way she'd be able to climb over the sides without help.

She wanted out of the ocean more than anything, but wasn't sure how to accomplish it.

"Uh, you guys wouldn't happen to have a ladder would you?"

Patrick smiled down at her for the first time since he'd arrived, as if she was a shining ray of sun in the rising morning fog. "Nope. Give me your hand."

Julie sighed. He was smiling, but his words were obviously an order. Still not meeting Cookie's eyes, Julie lifted one hand toward Patrick. He immediately grabbed hold of her wrist in a grip she knew she wouldn't slip out of. He had her. She was safe.

"Give Cookie your other hand. We'll lift you over the edge. No problem."

Julie looked at the other man for the first time since the boat pulled up next to her. She bit her cracked lip. Hell. He was holding his hand out toward her.

When their eyes met, he said simply, "It's okay. Trust me."

Shit. She raised her other hand and felt it, too, grasped in a secure grip. Before Julie could even think about how they were going to get her into the boat, she was there. The two men had lifted her as if she weighed five pounds instead of over a hundred. Then she was in Patrick's arms.

They'd set her on her feet on the bottom of the boat, but her knees had immediately given out. She would've crumpled to the floor, but Patrick was there. He wrapped his arms around her and eased her down, still holding her tight. Julie could feel the boat moving, but didn't lift her head. She was exhausted. She felt as if she could sleep for days.

Knowing she had to do it before she either lost her nerve or passed out, she raised her head to look for Cookie. She found him driving the boat, but alternating between watching where he was going, and looking down at her and his Commander.

"Thank you," Julie said without breaking eye contact with Cookie. "Thank you for coming to get me, for being patient with me. I know I was a bitch, and probably the worst rescued person you ever had to deal with. I was a selfish cow and I'm sorry. You probably don't believe me, but I'm working on being a better person. I swear, I'm not the same woman you met in Mexico."

"I know, and you're welcome."

"You know?" Julie asked, surprised and confused.

"Yeah. Hurt wouldn't put up with the bitch I met in Mexico. And since he likes you a heck of a lot, I figure you must've used what happened to you to better yourself."

"You're not pissed at me? I was horrible. And I also heard that you married Fiona...I don't—"

"Julie. Stop. Do I think you and Fee are ever gonna be best friends? No. Are we suddenly gonna go out and get manis and pedis together? Hell no. But I can appreciate that you were under a lot of stress while we were in that hellhole. Don't screw Hurt over, and we're cool. All right?"

Julie nodded and buried her head back in Patrick's neck. "I'm not going to screw you over," she told Patrick in a low voice, "but I can't promise to never be a bitch again. I think I have the gene. It's buried deep, but it's still there."

Patrick chuckled. "I can handle your bitch gene."

"Okay. Patrick?"

"Yeah, sweetheart?"

"Thank you for finding me. I was so scared."

"You did good, Julie. Except for the part where you dove into the middle of a rip current when I specifically told you to stay out of the water. We'll have to talk about that later."

Julie lifted her head and looked at Patrick. She spoke softly so Johnnie wouldn't hear. "There's no way he would've survived. The lifeguards were already all in the water trying to help others. There wasn't anyone else around to go after him."

Patrick didn't respond, but put his hand on the back of her head and returned it to his neck. He held her against him the entire way back to the beach. When they arrived, Cookie pulled the boat as close to shore as he could and Wolf carried the little boy out of the boat. The mother was there and grabbed hold of her child, who immediately started crying now that he was back in his mother's sympathetic arms.

"Where's your stuff?" Patrick asked Julie.

She lifted her head and looked toward where she'd left her stuff. She could see it over the edge of the boat and between the people milling around the crowded beach. "It's over there, next to the three police officers."

Wolf set off toward the men and Julie watched as he gathered up her stuff and headed back to the boat. Without a word, he climbed in and Cookie once again shoved the boat back into the water. The guys who were in the other boats followed behind. They'd been speaking with the lifeguards and the local police. Amazingly, everyone had been accounted for. Between the lifeguards and the SEALs, everyone was back on shore, safe and sound.

They took off back toward Coronado at a much slower pace than they'd left. Patrick still hadn't moved from the bottom of the boat, and thus Julie hadn't either.

The trip back was relatively silent until Wolf said, suddenly and somewhat bizarrely, "Does Johnnie know who you are, Julie?"

She raised her head and looked at Wolf. "What do you mean? He knows my name is Julie, but if you're asking if I gave my phone number to a five-year-old when we were treading water in the middle of the ocean, the answer is no."

"So his mom won't be able to find you to thank you."

"Probably not, unless she really digs. But so what? I didn't jump my ass into the ocean to get accolades. I did it to save Johnnie. He's what mattered He's a five-year-old kid who let his curiosity get the better of him. He made a mistake. He didn't do it on purpose." Julie was slightly miffed that Wolf would think she'd demand thanks from Johnnie's mother, until she saw the smile on his face. She looked over at Cookie who was driving, and he too was smiling.

She turned to Patrick, only to see a smile as big as she'd ever seen creep across his face as well. "What the hell are you all smiling about?"

"You didn't do it for thanks. You did it to save a life. Was it worth it?" Cookie asked.

Slowly Julie understood. "Yeah," she breathed, "it was worth it."

"So, you're welcome, Julie. You now know first-hand that we don't do what we do for thanks. We do it because it needs to be done. Just as you did today."

Cookie's words sank in, but Julie couldn't let it go completely. Almost, but not quite yet. "But sometimes, the person you saved *needs* to say thanks."

"Then say it so we can be done with it and we can all move on."

Julie smiled. She couldn't be pissed. "Then thank you, Cookie. And Wolf, thank you for getting my ass out of that hellhole."

"Again, you're welcome. Now we're done with that, yeah?" Wolf asked with mock impatience.

"We're done."

"Good."

"Relax, sweetheart," Patrick said into her ear as he pulled her into him again. "You've had a hard day, let me take care of you."

"I can do that." She smiled into Patrick's neck and let him take her weight. It felt right, being in his arms. She was where she was meant to be, and it was a pretty damn good place to end up.

CHAPTER 12

JULIE TRIED NOT TO HYPERVENTILATE. THE COMPANY picnic had been postponed; there was no way Patrick wanted to put any of the people under his command in danger. The rip current was gone, but no one wanted to take a chance on another while their families were enjoying a day at the beach.

After the boats had arrived at the training area at Coronado, Patrick had helped her to his office, sat her on a chair, and told her he'd be back in two minutes to take her home. He'd been true to his word. He'd returned and, without a word, picked her up, even though she'd insisted she could walk, and taken her back to his place.

She'd showered and put on a pair of his sweats, which were huge on her, and a SEAL T-shirt. Patrick had made her drink a full bottle of water to replace some of the fluids she'd lost out in the ocean, and they'd both crawled onto his bed even though it was only five o'clock in the afternoon.

Julie sighed, remembering how safe she'd felt wrapped in Patrick's arms, under his covers, wearing his clothes, snug as a bug in a rug. She'd fallen asleep and hadn't woken up until the next morning, when Patrick kissed her forehead before he'd gotten out of bed.

Apparently her conversation in the boat with Cookie and Wolf had indicated to Patrick that she was ready to talk to the rest of the team—and Fiona. He'd informed her, after another shower and while they were eating yogurt and bagels for breakfast that he'd arranged a team meeting that morning.

Julie had tried to protest, but Patrick had stopped her by asking two questions.

"Do you want to be with me? To see where this can go between us?"

Her answer was immediate. "Yes."

"Then we need to be there at ten. The guys will meet us there, and Fiona is coming over at ten-thirty."

So now it was time. Julie was sitting in a surprisingly comfortable chair in a large meeting room at

Patrick's building. The leather chair squeaked a bit as she shifted nervously and tried not to freak out and run screaming from the room. But she wanted this. She did. It was why she'd spoken to Stacey and Diesel back in Virginia in the first place. Why she'd wanted to track down the SEALs. She wanted to move on.

Patrick was sitting next to her, looking amazing in his battle dress uniform. Julie hadn't gotten to fully appreciate it the day before in the middle of her rescue. He was there to support her, to make sure his men didn't say or do anything that would hurt her further. He'd told her they wouldn't, but he was still there, having her back.

The door opened, and Julie watched as Cookie, Wolf, and four other men entered. Four sat in various chairs around the table in the room, while Cookie and one other man stayed standing, leaning against one of the walls.

Julie didn't beat around the bush; she started right in, deciding that drawing it out wasn't the best course of action for her rapidly beating heart and her psyche.

"Thank you for coming down to Mexico to rescue me. I know you did it because of my dad, but I appreciate it nonetheless. I've already had this talk with Cookie and Wolf, and I realize you probably don't need or want my thanks, but you have it anyway. I know it was your job, and you've done it before and you'll probably do it again, but please know that even though I looked unimpressed and acted like a selfish child, I appreciate it more than you'll know."

Julie then turned to Cookie. "And I said it to you yesterday, and I'll say it again today in front of your teammates. I'm sorry about how I acted. I was scared and hurting. That's no excuse, because I know Fiona was too and she didn't act like me. The thing I'm most ashamed of is trying to get you to leave that stupid hut without telling you someone else was there too." Julie looked down at her hands, clasped in her lap under the table. She dug her fingernails into her palms, trying to gather the courage to say what she needed to say. Patrick put his hand over hers and squeezed, letting her know he was there for her.

She looked up into Cookie's eyes. "It doesn't change anything that happened or anything I said or did, but I'm trying to be a better person."

Cookie put her out of her misery. "As I told you yesterday, Julie, you're welcome. I can't lie; you weren't the most enjoyable person to be with in the jungle, and I did have a hard time forgiving you for almost allowing me to leave Fiona there. But, she didn't get left. She's here, alive, and she's doing great. I don't need your thanks or your apology, but they're appreciated all the same."

Julie sagged in relief. Again, though they'd kind of already had this conversation yesterday in the boat, him accepting her apology and her thanks in front of his comrades somehow made it different. More official. She nodded at him, grateful.

The other man standing against the wall spoke up as well. "I'm Dude, and you're right, Julie. No thanks are necessary, but to be honest, it's nice to hear every once in a while." He came over to where she was sitting and held out his hand. Julie put hers into it and was surprised when he pulled her out of her chair and into his arms for a big bear hug. "I'm glad you're changing your life around."

The other men in the room also came over and hugged her, each accepting her thanks in a personal way. Afterwards, they filed out of the room. Finally, it was Cookie's turn. He put his hands on her shoulders and looked her in the eye. "You ready?"

Julie knew what he meant. She nodded.

He walked to the door and looked out and gestured to someone. Fiona came into view and Julie watched as Cookie took hold of her hand and held it as she entered the room. Cookie closed the door behind them.

Again, knowing she had to jump right in, Julie immediately apologized. "I'm sorry I was a bitch, Fiona. You did nothing but try to help me out there. You were gracious and even though you were suffering, you still tried to comfort me. I threw it in your face, making fun of your counting and even being greedy with the food. I played into your insecurities about not being the one they were there to rescue. It was inexcusable and I'm sorrier than you'll ever know." Julie's words were rushed, as if she thought Fiona would butt in and cut her off before she could get them out.

"Apology accepted," Fiona said easily.

Julie's eyes welled with tears and she bit her lip, trying to control herself. She felt Patrick's hand on her back, caressing and reassuring her.

Fiona went on. "I didn't expect to see you in your store. It was a shock and I didn't know what to think or feel. I think I owe *you* an apology for the way my friends handled the situation."

Julie began to interrupt her, but Fiona held up her hand. "Let me finish. In Caroline and Alabama's defense, I'd had a flashback when I got home after Mexico, and I took off. I thought I was back there, and there were men chasing me. No one knew where I was and I totally freaked my friends out. I know they thought seeing you would bring on another flashback and they only wanted to make sure I was safe. It wasn't really about you, Julie."

Julie shook her head sadly. "But they know about me."

Fiona nodded slowly. "Yeah. I told them some of what happened down there. It's what friends do."

It was Julie who nodded this time. "I know. I'll apologize to them too. I'll apologize to anyone you want me to, Fiona. I admire the hell out of you. You survived so much more than me. I wouldn't have been able to do it."

"Yes, you would. I was just like you, Julie. Exactly like you. At first I was ready and willing to do whatever they said so they'd stop hurting me and hopefully let me go. But slowly I realized they weren't going to let me go, so I started fighting them. You would've gotten to that point too. I know it. Look at you now. You have a will of steel. You not only braved Hunter and the other guys, but me too."

The two women smiled at each other. Julie knew they'd never be besties, but maybe, just maybe, they could be comfortable enough that seeing each other wouldn't cause old wounds to open and fester.

"Would it be all right if I stopped by your store sometime soon? I never did get to see all the awesome things you've got there, and I heard all about how great it was from Caroline after she went the first time."

"Of course. Anytime you want to come by, I'll be there. Just let me know, even if it's after hours."

"And you really do donate clothes to women's shelters and to teenagers who need a dress for a school dance and can't afford it?" Fiona asked, sounding somewhat impressed.

Julie nodded. "Uh-huh. I love the looks on their faces when they come out of the dressing room wearing a Vera Wang or Gucci dress and it's obvious they feel fabulous."

"I'd say you've come a long way since that bitch in the jungle."

Julie laughed, not offended in the least. "I hope so. I'm trying."

"You're succeeding."

"Thanks for giving me the chance to apologize, Fiona. Seriously."

"You're welcome."

"See you tomorrow, Hurt?" Cookie asked, shaking his Commander's hand.

"O-five-hundred for PT," Patrick confirmed.

Cookie nodded and he and Fiona left the room.

Julie felt herself being pulled back into Patrick's arms. He wrapped his arms around her from behind and held her cradled against his chest. "You okay?"

"Yeah. That was..." Her voice trailed off, unsure of the word she was looking for.

"Cathartic?"

It was as good a word as any to try to explain how she was feeling. She nodded and nuzzled her cheek against Patrick's shoulder. "Thank you for setting it up for me."

"You're welcome. It's what Tex sent you to me to do, after all."

Julie laughed. "Only a few months later than he expected it to happen though."

"True. You ready to go?"

"Yeah, I have some stuff I need to do at the store. I've been neglecting it too long. The people that work with me are good, but they hate the sales stuff. Daddy hired them because they're good at marketing and accounting. I need to set up a meeting with the director of a women's clinic and see who has interviews coming up and what I can do to help."

"In case I haven't told you already, you're amazing,"

Julie turned in Patrick's grasp, happy he kept his arms around her, and looked up. "It feels good to help people, rather than belittle them or make fun of them for what they don't have. It's what I've done in the past, and I'm ashamed of it."

Instead of responding to her words, Patrick said, "You're coming over tonight, right?"

Julie thought the change of subject was a bit bizarre, but she answered affirmatively anyway.

"Good. I enjoyed holding you in my arms last night. But I think it's time to move our relationship to the next level…if you're ready."

Julie knew exactly what Patrick was saying. She grinned up at him. "I'm definitely ready, and I'd like that."

"I have a meeting at four today, but I'm headed home right after. When can you get there?"

"Anxious, are you?" Julie teased.

"Hell yes. You have no idea what's in store for you tonight, sweetheart. I've dreamed about your body under mine. I've thought about how you'll sound when you come apart for me. All of it. I can't wait. And, as you heard me tell Cookie, I have PT in the morning, so you need to get to my place as soon as possible. I'm not planning on either of us getting much sleep."

Julie knew she had a stupid grin on her face, but she couldn't help it. "I'll make sure I'm there by five. That work?"

"Perfectly. And as much as I want to kiss the hell out of you right now, it's not exactly appropriate for the Commander of a Navy SEAL team to be sucking face at work. So for my professional reputation's sake, get going. I'll see you tonight."

Julie nodded and pulled back reluctantly. "Thank you for being you, Patrick."

He nodded. "Go on. Be safe."

Julie smiled at him and walked backward to the door, not turning around until she'd exited and couldn't see him anymore. The goofy grin on her face stayed there for most of the day.

CHAPTER 13

DINNER WAS DELICIOUS. THE DISHES WERE IN THE dishwasher and Julie was drying her hands on the dishtowel hanging off of the handle on the refrigerator. She'd turned to ask Patrick what else she could do when she found herself being lifted through the air. She screeched and grabbed on to Patrick's shoulders as she was spun around and her butt landed on the table they'd finished eating their meal on not ten minutes earlier.

"Patrick, what the—"

Her words were cut off when his mouth came down on hers and his tongue swept inside, making her lose whatever it was she was saying. She wrapped her legs around his hips and her hands went to his shoulders as she hung on for the ride.

Patrick couldn't wait anymore. He'd controlled himself throughout their pre-dinner small-talk and as they'd eaten. But watching her chew, and laugh, and generally just be the wonderful person she was, had pushed him over the edge.

When he'd watched Julie in his kitchen, happily helping him clean up the mess he'd made preparing the lasagna they'd eaten, something snapped inside.

He needed her. Now.

His hands wandered up her sides, wondering anew about how delicate she seemed. She was tiny compared to him, but her personality more than made up for her small stature. She felt as if she was made to be in his arms. Patrick picked his head up to look her in the eyes. "You ready for this? For me?" He wanted her to be one hundred percent sure. He knew what she'd been through, and they'd had a talk about this once. She'd reassured him that she didn't have any hang-ups about sex, but he needed to be certain. The last thing he wanted to do was traumatize her any more than she'd already been.

"Take me, Patrick. I want you."

It was all he needed to hear. His hands went to the bottom of the shirt she was wearing. It had buttons down the front, but they would take too long to bother with. He drew it upward and Julie lifted her arms to assist him as he pulled it over her head. Patrick threw it behind him without looking. He'd had his lips on her tits in the past, and couldn't wait to suck on them again, but for now he needed more. He needed to be inside her.

His hands went to the button on her pants, but her hands were already there.

"I'll get this. You do yours." Julie's voice was breathy and urgent.

Patrick liked the way she thought. He grabbed his wallet out of his pocket and quickly pulled the condom out. He'd put it there earlier, so it was handy. Holding the packet between his teeth, he quickly undid the button on his jeans and lowered the zipper, never taking his eyes off of Julie's fingers as she did the same to her own pants.

Patrick quickly rolled the condom over his erection and helped Julie pull one leg out of her jeans and panties. He didn't give her a chance to remove them completely. He put his hand over her folds and sighed at the wetness he found there. He put his other hand on her belly, amazed how his entire hand could almost span her from hip bone to hip bone.

"God, you're small," he said, for the first time worrying about her size compared to his.

"You'll fit, Patrick," Julie reassured him, putting her hands over her head and arched her back.

Her wanton pose made him groan. He held her still as his fingers caressed and teased her bundle of nerves and her soaking-wet folds. Never giving her what she was so greedily asking for. "All I could think of while you were eating tonight was laying you out on this table and fucking you so hard you'd feel me for days."

"Then what are you waiting for? Do it!" Julie demanded in exasperation.

"Because now that I have you right here where I'd fantasized about, I've decided I want to go slow, to take my time. I realize I should carry you into my bedroom and take you on my bed, you deserve that and more. But if I have to wait another second to make you mine, I don't know what I'll do."

"Fuck me, Patrick," Julie moaned. "Please, for the love of God, stop teasing me and take me."

Before the last word was out of her mouth, Patrick put one hand next to her hip on the table and guided the tip of his condom-covered cock to her opening with the other.

They both groaned as he entered her for the first time.

"Oh lord, Julie. You're so hot and slick."

"More, give me more!"

Patrick pulled back then pushed in a little farther than he'd been in before. "Slowly, Julie. I want this to be slow. I don't want to hurt you, but I also want to savor it." He put one hand on the back of her neck, making sure she was looking at him. Both of her hands latched on to his waist and she whimpered passionately under him, gazing up at him and breathing hard.

He pulled out and eased inside her a bit farther and held still. "I love you, Julie Lytle. I want to be the only man you let in here for the rest of your life. I want to protect you from anyone who tries to hurt you and be there when you need me. I want to fuck you on my table, on the couch, on the counter, in my shower and in my bed. I don't think I'll ever get enough of you."

Without giving her time to respond, Patrick pushed the rest of the way inside. He ground his hips against hers, loving how she immediately lifted her legs and wrapped them around him, her actions showing him more than words ever could that she was over what had happened to her all those months ago. He could feel her jeans dangling off of one of her legs and his own pants were hanging off his ass. He hadn't even taken the time to take off his shirt.

But even with both of them still half-dressed, Patrick still felt more naked than he had in his entire life as he waited for Julie's reaction to his words.

"Yes, Patrick. I love you too. I have no idea how I got lucky enough to be here, with you, with everything I've done and who I've been in the past, but I'll fight and die to keep it now. To keep *you*."

Patrick groaned, pulled back and thrust back inside Julie, hard. His hands slapped on the table next to her, balancing him over her. He'd wanted to keep this soft and light. To slowly bring them both to an orgasm, but it didn't look as if that was going to happen. Oh, the orgasm would happen, but instead of being a gentle, loving thing, it was going to be hard and explosive. Patrick could already feel the stirrings of it moving over him.

He stood upright abruptly, holding onto Julie's hips and pulling her into him, angling her so that her hips were tilted upward to take his cock but her back was still on the table. He slammed into her once, then twice.

"Oh yeah, that feels amazing," Julie moaned, grabbing hold of both sides of the small square table with her hands, bracing herself for his thrusts. "Again, do it again, Patrick."

Patrick shifted one hand so his thumb could press against her clit as he pistoned in and out of her small body. He felt her body grip him harder as he drew back, as if she didn't want to let him go. Then he pushed through her quaking muscles back inside to heaven.

He'd had plenty of sex in his life, but Patrick didn't remember any of those encounters being like this. He flicked his thumb faster over Julie's bundle of nerves. "Come on, sweetheart. I wanna see you explode for me. That's it...right there. Oh yeah."

Patrick watched as Julie's back arched off the table, her mouth opened with only a groan escaping, and she jerked in his grasp. She humped her hips against his own as her orgasm washed over her. He felt her muscles fluttering around his cock and the rush of wetness against his balls as she thrashed in ecstasy.

He waited until she pulled away from his thumb, which he'd kept on her clit, prolonging her orgasm. She'd reached the point where it wasn't pleasurable anymore because of how sensitive her clit was. Patrick put both hands on the table and leaned over her.

"That was beautiful. Abso-fucking-lutely beauti-ful. Hold on to me. Watch as you take me over too."

Patrick felt Julie's hands slide under his shirt and latch onto his hips.

"I'm gonna take you hard. You ready?"

"Oh yeah. Do it. Fuck me, Patrick."

It was if her words flicked a switch inside of him. He couldn't hold back any longer. He looked down and watched as his cock disappeared into her body, then reappeared, then disappeared again as he sank into her warm body. "I'm coming...oh God, Julie!" Patrick thrust two more times, hard, and held himself deep as he came. The world narrowed to Julie and the feel of her under him as he emptied himself deep inside her.

He came back to himself and opened his eyes, not realizing at some point he'd closed them, to see Julie smiling up at him. She was running her hands over his sides soothingly, patiently waiting for him to come back to his senses.

"Holy shit," Patrick whispered reverently.

"I think that's my line," Julie teased.

Patrick leaned over and grabbed Julie with one hand around her waist and the other behind her back. She squealed in surprise as he once again easily picked her up.

"Hold on tight."

She did as he asked and Patrick shuffled through his house to his bedroom, trying not to trip over his pants, which had slid down to his knees. He heard Julie giggle as he almost tripped. He made it to his bedroom and stopped by the bed.

"Drop your legs, sweetheart."

"I don't want to lose you."

Her words made his heart swell. "Unfortunately, as much as I might want it, I can't spend the rest of our lives with my cock inside you, as good as it feels. I have to deal with this condom and we have to get these fucking clothes off. I promise, Julie, as soon as I'm up and ready again, I'll be right back in there. But in the meantime, I have time to learn every inch of your body, to taste you, to lick you, to make you mine."

"I *am* yours, Patrick. As long as you want me."

"That's good then, because I want you forever."

She eased her grip on his hips and he pulled back, allowing her to drop her legs to the ground. "Strip."

Within minutes, he'd taken care of the used condom, removed his clothes, and joined Julie in his bed, both of them naked.

"I'm sorry our first time wasn't romantic," Patrick

apologized ruefully. "I meant for it to be, but as I told you out there—"

Julie cut off his words. "It was perfect. I rather like that you wanted me so badly you couldn't wait."

"It's a good thing. I have a feeling it's going to be that way a lot."

Julie only grinned up at him and said, "Now... about those other things you said you were going to do...you better get to work...five o'clock is going to come awfully early in the morning."

Patrick mock saluted her and scooted down her body, easing her legs apart and settling in. "Yes, ma'am. Anything you say."

———

If you haven't read *Protecting Fiona*, where Julie was first introduced, you should do that. :) You'll have a much better appreciation for what Julie had to apologize for.

JOIN my Newsletter and find out about sales, free books, contests and new releases before anyone else!! Click HERE

Want to know when my books go on sale? Follow me on Bookbub HERE!

Would you like Susan's Book Protecting Caroline for FREE?
Click HERE

Rescuing Rayne

Rescuing Aimee (novella)

Rescuing Emily

Rescuing Harley

Marrying Emily

Rescuing Kassie

Rescuing Bryn

Rescuing Casey

Rescuing Sadie

Rescuing Wendy

Rescuing Mary (Oct 2018)

Rescuing Macie (April 2019)

Badge of Honor: Texas Heroes Series

Justice for Mackenzie

Justice for Mickie

Justice for Corrie

Justice for Laine (novella)

Shelter for Elizabeth

Justice for Boone

Shelter for Adeline

Shelter for Sophie

Justice for Erin

Justice for Milena

Shelter for Blythe

Justice for Hope (Sept 2018)

Shelter for Quinn (Feb 2019)
Shelter for Koren (June 2019)
Shelter for Penelope (Oct 2019)

Ace Security Series

Claiming Grace
Claiming Alexis
Claiming Bailey
Claiming Felicity

Mountain Mercenaries Series

Defending Allye (Aug 2018)
Defending Chloe (Dec 2018)
Defending Morgan (Mar 2019)
Defending Harlow (July 2019)
Defending Everly (TBA)
Defending Zara (TBA)
Defending Raven (TBA)

Stand Alone

The Guardian Mist
Nature's Rift
A Princess for Cale
A Moment in Time- A Collection of Short Stories
Lambert's Lady

Special Operations Fan Fiction

http://www.stokeraces.com/kindle-worlds.html

Beyond Reality Series

Outback Hearts

Flaming Hearts

Frozen Hearts

Writing as Annie George:

Stepbrother Virgin (erotic novella)

ABOUT THE AUTHOR

New York Times, *USA Today* and *Wall Street Journal* Bestselling Author Susan Stoker has a heart as big as the state of Tennessee where she lives, but this all American girl has also spent the last eighteen years living in Missouri, California, Colorado, Indiana, and Texas. She's married to a retired Army man who now gets to follow *her* around the country.

She debuted her first series in 2014 and quickly followed that up with the SEAL of Protection Series, which solidified her love of writing and creating stories readers can get lost in.

If you enjoyed this book, or any book, please consider leaving a review. It's appreciated by authors more than you'll know.

www.stokeraces.com
susan@stokeraces.com

facebook.com/authorsusanstoker

twitter.com/Susan_Stoker

instagram.com/authorsusanstoker

goodreads.com/SusanStoker

bookbub.com/authors/susan-stoker

amazon.com/author/susanstoker

Printed in Great Britain
by Amazon

67749523R00092